Books by Tom Ballard

Fiction

- **The President is Down** (Novel)
  The most powerful man in the world crashes in Central America where a beautiful peasant rescues him from rebels, soldiers, and himself.

- **The Last Quack** (Novel)
  Kate Turner, naturopathic physician, discovers that tripping over a dead body may be hazardous to her health, especially when the dead woman was researching the same medicinal mushroom.

- **Eco-Agent Man: the case of the vanishing moth** (Film Script)
  Nick Chronos, undercover Ecology-Agent with a bag of quirky low-tech tricks, battles a ruthless developer to save an endangered species – the Spotted Porch Light Moth.

- **Get to Know your Duck** (Play)
  The Bland family's complacent existence is scrambled when the twins bring home a two-headed duck that keeps growing... and growing...

Non-Fiction

- **Pure Weight Loss: Patient Guide**
  The future of health and weight loss

- **Nutrition-1-2-3: three diet wisdoms for losing weight, gaining energy, and reversing aging**
  The basics of natural nutrition for shopping, eating and regaining your health

Get To Know Your Duck

A Play

Tom Ballard

Fresh Press Books
3315 59th Ave. SW
Seattle, WA 98116
(206)679-9417
FreshPressBooks@gmail.com

The characters and duck in this story are entirely fictional. Any resemblance to persons or ducks living or dead is coincidental. No ducks were harmed in the making of this play.

Get To Know Your Duck

Tom Ballard

ISBN 1449537731

EAN-13 9781449537739

Author photo by Patsy Hilbert

Get To Know Your Duck

Synopsis

Get To Know Your Duck is a comedy set in a near-future when every family keeps a Smog-O-Matic by the front door.

The Bland family lives in deep denial of the environmental disasters around them and the green slime that oozes through the walls. Steven Bland believes in positive thinking and is loyal to his employer, Cow Chemical. Constance Bland cleans house cheerfully and constantly, while fretting about her inability to have more children. The Twins repeat everything that's said to them, crave sweets and remind their mother when she forgets their names (They are played by an off-stage actor who speaks through puppets. The audience sees only the back of the twins' heads as they sit on a couch watching TV)

The Blands' routine is soon scrambled by a series of calamities starting with the Twins bringing home a giant egg from the swamp (Yes, the swamp owned by Cow Chemical!) The egg soon hatches a two-headed duck that starts growing . . . and growing.

With the help of the local eco-radical, Professor Chalk, the Blands discover the putrid swamp is causing infertility, malocclusions, and the still-growing duck.

Constance's awakening prompts her to stop cleaning and take control of the T.V. news from pompous reporter Clara Fry.

Steven is reluctant to believe anything negative about his boss, Mr. Cow, until he learns of Cow's plans for duck pâté. He's soon confronting Cow and Agent Orange, from the EPA. The duck-napping is foiled with the help of the duck who chases away the police S.Q.A.T team (by this time the duck is so big, only its giant legs can be seen through the living-room window)

The duck is saved, the world alerted, and, although Steven loses his job, he gains a wife with a brain and a duck as big as a house.

The eight character (six actor) play takes place entirely in the Bland's living room and requires the imaginative use of puppets (or a large, trained, two-headed duck).

Get To Know Your Duck, is a sort of An Enemy of the People for the 21st Century, with feathers.

Get to Know your Duck

Our action begins...

GET TO KNOW YOUR DUCK
ACT I, SCENE 1

(CONSTANCE, a frazzled-looking woman in her late 30's is ironing clothes, and everything is sight, including sheets and socks, with rapid, staccato precision. The backs of the TWINS heads are seen on the couch)

TV ANNOUNCER
Tonight's weather calls for increasing low clouds and high pressure and we all know what that means---air inversion. If you must go outside, a pure-air mask and compass are recommended. But, don't despair, your weekend plans should not be disrupted. Tomorrow's weather is expected to improve with visibility increasing to the normal 30 feet. And now, sports...

TWINS (They always speak in unison)
Mommy. Mommy.

CONSTANCE
Yes, uhm,...Lucy and Dezy.

(CONSTANCE pulls a comb out of apron and sets to work on TWINS hair)

TWINS
Timmy, Timmy. Sally, Sally.

CONSTANCE
Oh, yes, (to herself) God, what's happening to me? (To Twins) What is it Timmy and Sally?

TWINS
Baby chant, baby chant.

Get to Know your Duck

CONSTANCE

That's right! Uhm...Fred and Ethel, time for my affirmations. (Sits on floor in lotus position, deep breathing) My uterus is round. My uterus is soft and full of life. My uterus is round and open...

(STEVEN ENTERS. With him comes a cloud of smog)

STEVEN

(Cough, hack) I'm home.

TWINS

Daddy! Daddy!

STEVEN

Hi, Sally and Timmy.

CONSTANCE

(Distressed) Oh! Oh!

(CONSTANCE runs to entrance, takes up her SMOG-O-Matic (a modified leaf-blowing machine) turns it on and blows the smog back outside)

STEVEN

(Shouting over blower) Hello, Constance.

(STEVEN removes coat and hat which releases a cloud of dust. CONSTANCE turns the blower on him, forcing the dust outside. She then slams the door and turns off the blower)

CONSTANCE

Hello, sweetie.

Get to Know your Duck

(They kiss. CONSTANCE returns to her ironing. STEVEN attempts to hang up his coat and hat, but they fall on the floor)

TWINS
Daddy! Daddy! Bring us something? Bring us something?

STEVEN
(Messing up their hair) No, I'm sorry.

TWINS
Oh nuts. Oh nuts.

STEVEN
Sorry. What did you do today?

TWINS
Play, play.

CONSTANCE
(Scolding) Do you want to know what they did today?

STEVEN
(He doesn't want to hear bad news) Ah, it sounds like I don't.

CONSTANCE
They snuck down to that dirty old swamp.

STEVEN
(To Constance) I knew I didn't want to hear. (To Twins) You know you're not supposed to go near the swamp, it's dangerous.

TWINS
Egg, egg.

(Steven takes large EGG from the Twins.)

Get to Know your Duck

STEVEN
Looks like an egg.

TWINS
Too big. Too big.

STEVEN
I wouldn't know about that. But didn't I tell you not to bring anything from outside into the house unless mommy cleaned it first? Especially anything from the swamp. Remember that stain your pet frog left on the carpet?

TWINS
Croak, croak.

CONSTANCE
It's not funny.

TWINS
Croak, croak.

STEVEN
Don't tease your mother. (Inspecting the egg) Are we having omelets for dinner, dear?

CONSTANCE
Don't be gross, you know that came from nature.

TWINS
Too big. Too big.

STEVEN
Well, what's new in the world?

(STEVEN sits and snaps open the NEWSPAPER, some of which falls on floor. CONSTANCE automatically picks up after him. STEVEN doesn't notice)

Get to Know your Duck

STEVEN (cont.)
(As he discards sections of the newspaper, unread) No...No...Not that... No...Definitely not...(Only one section remains) Ah, here we go, sports.

TWINS
T.V., T.V.

(T.V. volume increases)

TV ANNOUNCER
In other news tonight: The Senate is scheduled to hold hearings on environmental cleanup Monday. Democrats say something must be done. Republicans say something must be done. Next: Sports. But first these words from our sponsor.

(SEVERAL VOICES)
Hey, my headache's gone, my head's clear and I can breathe again.
Say, Ed, how do you keep your grass so green and your car so shiny?
I have a secret. My family thinks this bread is home made, but I bought it six months ago.

(ANNOUNCER)
In your home, in your factory and in your closet, your future is our future and the future is chemistry. The Cow Chemical Company, chemists to the world.

TWINS
Daddy's Cow. Daddy's Cow.

STEVEN
(With pride) That's right. Cow Chemical is where daddy works.
(Constance combs his hair)

CONSTANCE
How was your day, dear?

STEVEN
Great. Lots of activity. You know Cow Chemical, making the world better. How was your day?

Get to Know your Duck

CONSTANCE
Fine, fine. I washed the children's toys and dusted the plants.

TWINS
Chirp, chirp.

CONSTANCE
(Pointing to an empty birdcage) Oh, yes, and do you want to know what happened to the canary?

STEVEN
Oh, God, don't say it.

TWINS
Canary go plop. Canary go plop.

STEVEN
Not again. I must buy a replacement canary once a month.

CONSTANCE
I guess they're too frail.

STEVEN
They come with one foot in the pet cemetery.

CONSTANCE
Momma says they don't make birds like they used to.

STEVEN
I don't know why not, it must be easy enough to make a canary. Is it...did you...?

CONSTANCE
It's wrapped in tissue next to the toilet.

TWINS
Plop, flush. Plop, flush.

Get to Know your Duck

STEVEN
Oh, I hate that. Don't you think a dog is enough pet? Where is Radon? Radon!

RADON
(Radon is a ragged stuffed dog that never moves) Cough, wheeze.

STEVEN
Down boy. (Radon has not moved) Speak!

RADON
Cough, wheeze.

TWINS
Bow-wow. Bow-wow.

STEVEN
Has he been outside again?

CONSTANCE
I don't know.

TWINS
Swamp. Swamp.

STEVEN
Good boy. Protecting Timmy and Sally. Didn't I tell you that a genetically engineered, full-blooded Doberman guard dog would earn his keep? Right Radon?

RADON
Cough, wheeze.

TWINS
Pills, pills.

<h1 style="text-align:center">Get to Know your Duck</h1>

CONSTANCE
That's right, and I went to the drugstore to have my prescriptions filled.

STEVEN
Weren't you there yesterday?

CONSTANCE
Yes, I think so. I called Dr. Golf this morning and he prescribed a new medication for the ear numbness I've been having since I started that last pill.

STEVEN
The one for your fainting spells?

CONSTANCE
(Consulting a piece of paper) I think that was taken care of by my pink pill. This was the green pill I took for the purple rash on my knees that was caused by the red pill reacting with the blue pill. The blue pill is the one that helps me sleep so that I'm rested enough to take the yellow pill. The yellow pill must always be taken with the round white pill.

STEVEN
The white pill was your original pill?

CONSTANCE
(Unsure) Yes.

STEVEN
And your original problem was...

CONSTANCE
Uh...

STEVEN
That's right, bloating caused by the infertility pill. Remember to do your affirmations?

Get to Know your Duck

CONSTANCE
Uh...yes. I think so.

STEVEN
(Worried about her. But afraid to bring up an unpleasant subject) Constance...uhm...never mind. Oh, I'm sorry, I forgot, I have to work overtime this weekend.

CONSTANCE
Oh no! This weekend?

STEVEN
Just tomorrow.

CONSTANCE
No. I mean, Oh no! I mean, why now?'

(During her anxiety attack CONSTANCE runs around the room compulsively cleaning)

STEVEN
(Following Constance) It is quite an honor, I was asked personally by Mr. Cow.

CONSTANCE
Oh, no.

STEVEN
What's the matter? It's only a Saturday.

CONSTANCE
It's our time.

STEVEN
(Looking at his watch) Time?

CONSTANCE
(Cleaning the face of his watch) Our time.

Get to Know your Duck

STEVEN
(Getting it) Oh, you mean...?

CONSTANCE
Baby time! I'm going into ovulation, I'm fertile. We have an appointment with Dr. Golf tomorrow at 10am.

STEVEN
Really? I'm sorry. That's wonderful! I mean, well, I'm sorry. You know me, I just can't say n...n...n...

TWINS
No, no. No, no.

STEVEN
You know my motto, "Just say yes."

CONSTANCE
Every time I try to get pregnant something goes wrong. Last month ...(thinking)

TWINS
Cluck, cluck, spot, spot.

CONSTANCE
The twins had chicken pox. And the month before that....

TWINS
Kaboom, kaboom!

CONSTANCE
... the toilet exploded. And Dr. Golf says my biological clock is running out!

STEVEN
I'm sorry, dear. Next time I'll say n...n...n...(he can't say no)

Get to Know your Duck

TWINS
No, no. No, no.

CONSTANCE
How about if we go to bed early tonight? If you know what I mean. (She puts her arm around him)

STEVEN
You mean...?

CONSTANCE
You know what I mean. We'll just snuggle up and uh, well, get that sample, if you know what I mean.

STEVEN
I think I know what you mean.

CONSTANCE
And in the morning I can go and see Dr. Golf with, ah, it?

STEVEN
Without me?

CONSTANCE
Yes, he's just going to take the, uh, you know, stuff and squirt them, uh, inside me. Your little squirt will be with me.

STEVEN
Oh? It doesn't seem natural without me there with you, and Dr. Golf, and the nurse.

CONSTANCE
A little part of you will be there with me, and Dr. Golf, and the nurse.

Get to Know your Duck

STEVEN
(Recovering) I guess we don't have a choice if Cow Chemical, chemist to the world, needs me.

CONSTANCE
Just like old times.

STEVEN
Like old times?

CONSTANCE
Yes, you and me and the specimen container.

> (They put their arms over each other's shoulders and go toward the Twins)

CONSTANCE & STEVEN
(Sigh) Aren't they sweet.

TWINS
Back off. Back off.

> (They lean over the couch and each kiss a Twin)

TWINS (cont.)
Slop, slop. Yuck, yuck.

CONSTANCE
Why does Cow Chemical, the chemist in our car, want you at work tomorrow?

Get to Know your Duck

STEVEN
The company is planning on selling off the swamp on Monday. I'm meeting with the man from the Environmental Protection Agency to make sure all the papers are in order.

CONSTANCE
Why you? Couldn't Mr. Cow...?

STEVEN
The law doesn't allow the C.E.O. of a corporation to sign off on an E.P.A audit. To give the appearance of impartiality, a lackey must sign the papers.

CONSTANCE
I thought Mr. Sheep was the Chief Lackey.

STEVEN
Mr. Sheep is on vacation. (Proudly) And as Chief Under Lackey...

CONSTANCE
Why the big hurry, couldn't it be done on regular time?

STEVEN
For the sale to go through they must cover up the swamp. Bulldozers are coming Sunday to fill it in.

CONSTANCE
At last! Now the Twins won't be going down there and getting all dirty.

TWINS
Croak. Croak.

STEVEN
Don't tease your mother.

CONSTANCE
But why are they selling it?

Get to Know your Duck

STEVEN
I'm sure they have good reason. My boss insisted I get it done by tomorrow. Top priority, he said. Get it ready to sell, he said. Drop everything else, he said.

CONSTANCE
Why?

STEVEN
He didn't say.

CONSTANCE
Selling that disgusting swamp? What would anyone want with that mess?

STEVEN
Once it's covered, condominiums can be built on it.

CONSTANCE
Will they be able to get rid of the putrid odor?

STEVEN
I suppose.

CONSTANCE
And stop the water from bursting into flames whenever there's a lightening storm?

STEVEN
Oh course. Cow Chemical knows its business.

CONSTANCE
(Sulking)I don't think I like Cow Chemical, the chemist in our bedroom, interfering with my fertility cycle.

Get to Know your Duck

STEVEN
Constance! Remember, if it wasn't for Cow Chemical's pharmaceutical division, you wouldn't have a fertility cycle.

CONSTANCE
Oh! That's right.

(The doorbell rings)

RADON (Always the same)
Coughs, wheeze.

STEVEN
Down boy.

(CONSTANCE opens door)

CONSTANCE
Daddy.

(SHERIFF enters, uninvited)

RADON
Cough, wheeze.

TWINS
Visitor, visitor.

(CONSTANCE blows smog outside)

Get to Know your Duck

<u>STEVEN</u>
Oh, hi, sheriff. What brings you...

<u>SHERIFF</u>
(He only addresses Steven) Police business. What are you two doing?

<u>STEVEN</u>
Just discussing my work, I guess.

<u>SHERIFF</u>
That's good. Kids, there's a problem.

<u>STEVEN</u>
Do we have to know about it?

<u>SHERIFF</u>
Ah, cow chips, it's for your own good.

<u>STEVEN</u>
I was afraid of that.

<u>SHERIFF</u>
I gotta tell you that there's a mad man on the loose.

<u>STEVEN</u>
Oh no! Don't tell me he's dangerous.

<u>SHERIFF</u>
He's dangerous.

<u>STEVEN</u>
I asked you not to...

<u>SHERIFF</u>
You heard that I did.

Get to Know your Duck

STEVEN
Yes, sir. Sorry.

SHERIFF
Professor Chalk's the name. Know him?

STEVEN
Kind of, he lives up the street, always wears a trench coat.

SHERIFF
That's him. Under that trench coat he has a megaphone.

CONSTANCE
(Appalled) I wouldn't know anything about that.

STEVEN
Don't tell me he's...

SHERIFF
The worst kind of pervert there is.

CONSTANCE
You mean...

SHERIFF
Yea, a trespasser.

CONSTANCE
(Screams runs to twins and covers their eyes) My babies, you don't think my babies saw anything disgusting, do you?

SHERIFF
Might have. He's been trespassing on private property. Cow Chemical guards saw him snooping around the plant today. They think he might be planning some sort of terrorist act.

Get to Know your Duck

STEVEN
A terrorist? Why would anyone...?

SHERIFF
Sheep droppings! You better get your butt into church more often, son. Hell in a hand basket. Terrorists everywhere these days. No one's safe.

STEVEN
Did he do something?

SHERIFF
Not yet, but I'm sure he'll try. I've been keeping my eye on him for years. He's a misfit. A loner. You know, a college professor.

STEVEN
Gee, he always seemed nice enough.

SHERIFF
Dog doodoo, son, save your sympathy, he's probably around somewhere stirring up trouble, fermenting the devil's brew.

STEVEN
Sorry. Devil's brew?

SHERIFF
Ideas. He's full of ideas. He worships thinking. I checked the courthouse, figured he'd be there protesting something. No sign of him or his megaphone.

CONSTANCE
Mega...?

STEVEN
But, what's there to protest?

Get to Know your Duck

CONSTANCE
Daddy... (She straightens and brushes off his uniform while he ignores her)

SHERIFF
You wouldn't believe it, Steven, but that man can always dig up something to protest; water pollution, air pollution, food contamination, radiation, nuclear war, belly aching about something that's none of his business. He doesn't see that all of it is God's gift for us to bulldoze and reform in the image of our creator. Do you hear what I'm saying?

STEVEN
Yes, sir. He can't leave well enough alone.

SHERIFF
Exactly. You're absolutely right.

STEVEN
I've seen him going into the library a lot.

SHERIFF
See what I mean.

CONSTANCE
Daddy...

STEVEN
What's the use of complaining? Things are good. Right?

SHERIFF
Right. I don't know about you, but I try and remember that God made man first, then girls, then trees and mountains and all the other rubble. Besides, Chalk seems to have finally had a complete meltdown. You wouldn't believe what I saw in his house. In his basement he's got a whole bunch of science kinds of stuff and cages with mice!

Get to Know your Duck

TWINS
Squeak, squeak, squeak, squeak.

SHERIFF
Mice in cages! Makes you wonder, doesn't it?

STEVEN
(Without a clue) Goodness, mice in cages!

CONSTANCE
Daddy...(She begins combing his hair)

SHERIFF
(Jerking away) Mice droppings! Don't you get it? He probably does all kinds of filthy, unnatural things with them soft, fury, squirmy, little critters with their ticklish little whiskers.

CONSTANCE
Oh?

STEVEN
Whiskers...yea!

SHERIFF
Steven, you're here next to the swamp. I want you to keep on the lookout. If you see Chalk snooping around, call me right away.

STEVEN
Certainly, sir.

SHERIFF
I'm counting on you! Cow Chemical is counting on you.

STEVEN
Cow Chemical can always count on me.

Get to Know your Duck

CONSTANCE
I don't have to look do I?

SHERIFF
(As always, oblivious to her, he grabs Steven by the shirt and lifts him) Keep your door locked and stay away from him. He might look harmless, but he's a dangerous man.

CONSTANCE
Daddy...

SHERIFF
(Releasing Steven) OK, I'm off. (Pointing to Constance's belly) Constance, got something in the oven yet?

CONSTANCE
(Looking toward the kitchen) I don't think so. Do you smell something burning?

SHERIFF
So long. Remember, don't take any chances. You're lives might depend on it.

STEVEN
Nothing to worry about here.

(SHERIFF EXITS)

TWINS
Oink. Oink.

CONSTANCE
Sigh. (Her father has ignored her again)

Get to Know your Duck

STEVEN
That was nice of your father to stop by and warn us. He's so considerate, don't you think?

CONSTANCE
Yes.

STEVEN
(Acting tough) That Chalk better not come near my family.

CONSTANCE
OK, kids, run wash your hands for dinner.

TWINS
Feet hurt. Feet hurt.

STEVEN
(To Constance) How could their feet hurt? We just finished paying off the Podiatrist for those orthotic things for their fallen arches.

CONSTANCE
Let them rest, dears, I'll massage them later.

STEVEN
What a day, first the canary...

CONSTANCE
What happened to the canary?

STEVEN
The canary died, remember? (She doesn't) Never mind. Then the specimen...

CONSTANCE
What specimen?

Get to Know your Duck

STEVEN
You know, the little squirt.

CONSTANCE
Uh, can we, uh, can we start working on that little squirt soon?

STEVEN
Soon? It's not due till tomorrow.

CONSTANCE
Yes, but...well, it can, uh...

STEVEN
What? Can what?

CONSTANCE
Sometimes, not always, of course, but sometimes it...takes...a...little.....

STEVEN
What are you saying?

CONSTANCE
Nothing. Only sometimes it take...a...little...tiimmee.

STEVEN
There's nothing wrong with me.

CONSTANCE
Oh, I know, it's much better than when it took no time.

STEVEN
No time?

CONSTANCE
I mean, it's very...romantic, that you can go so long without... e..eliminating anything.

Get to Know your Duck

STEVEN

Romantic?

CONSTANCE

Yes, oh yes, ever since you took those pills Dr. Golf gave you, not that I minded before, I always thought it proved you loved me when you would squirt so fast, but now it's...different, now you just stays inside and wait and it doesn't seem like anything is happening, no one would suspect there was anything happening and then, well it starts and after a while it just oozes out, as if from nowhere, it is... romantic.

STEVEN

Romantic?

CONSTANCE

Yes, and...time consuming. Maybe we could put the twins to bed early.

TWINS

No, no. T.V. T.V.

STEVEN

Now, now, it would be a special favor for mommy and daddy.

TWINS

No way. No way. Bribe. Bribe.

STEVEN

Alright. I'll open the bidding with ice cream.

TWINS

Chocolate. Chocolate.

STEVEN

That's fair. It's a deal.

TWINS

Pie. Pie.

Get to Know your Duck

STEVEN
Oh, pie too? Well, if you want.

TWINS
Mmm. Mmm. Slurp. Slurp.

STEVEN
(To Constance) It's settled then. I'll run down to the Cow Shop and pick up some chocolate Cow Cream and a Cow pie.

CONSTANCE
Thank you dear.

STEVEN
I'll be back soon.

CONSTANCE
Straighten your tie dear and don't forget your gas mask.

STEVEN
Be back soon. And, remember, keep the door locked.

CONSTANCE
Locked?

STEVEN
Because of the mad-man terrorist.

CONSTANCE
Oh! Yes, dear.

(STEVEN EXITS)

Get to Know your Duck

CONSTANCE
(Looking around) Goodbye. Now, Mommy was going to do something...

TWINS
Chomp, chomp, munch, munch.

CONSTANCE
That's right, dinner. Thanks Peter and Laurie.

TWINS
Sally, Sally. Timmy, Timmy.

(Lights out)

ACT I, SCENE 2
(We see a greenish sunset through the window. Lights up on living room. In the background sirens can be heard (noise pollution). TWINS watching TV)

TV ANNOUNCER
Senate hearings are scheduled for Monday on the establishment of a Super Mega-fund for use in cleaning up industrial waste. Environmentalist call the vote crucial for the future of the planet. Critics call the bill a boondoggle for unnecessary frills such as air, water and earth. In weather, tonight air-smudge report calls for increasing parts-per-million of hydroputrazines. Pure air masks are recommended if you have to outside. Next, sports. But first...(another voice)
Hi, kids. Want to buy some swell toys and lots of gooey candy?

(Loud knocking at the door)

Get to Know your Duck

RADON
Cough, wheeze.

CONSTANCE
(Looking in from kitchen) Not so much noise … kids.

(Louder knocking at the door)

RADON
Cough, wheeze.

TWINS
Door. Door.

CONSTANCE
Oh!

(CONSTANCE crosses to door and is about to open it)

TWINS
Trespasser. Trespasser.

CONSTANCE
(She stops) Oh! That's right! Only open the door for Steven. (Through door) Steven?

VOICE (OS)
Cough, cough, hack, wheeze.

RADON
Cough, wheeze.

Get to Know your Duck

TWINS
Bark. Bark.

CONSTANCE
Oh! That's not daddy's cough! Hide!

TWINS
Pigs! Pigs!

CONSTANCE
Yes, I'll call the police!

>(CONSTANCE tiptoes toward the phone but is distracted by newspapers on the floor and is quickly caught up in house cleaning which keeps her near door)

(LOUD KNOCKING)

CONSTANCE (cont.)
Oh! Steven?

RADON
Cough, wheeze

>(CONSTANCE, without thinking, opens the door. CHALK stumbles in coughing and wheezing. He wears a trench coat with various protest buttons and carries a megaphone strapped over his shoulder)

CONSTANCE
(SCREAMS) Stop, it's disgusting! Please don't open your coat! Get that disgusting thing away from my children!

>(CONSTANCE runs to TWINS and covers their eyes, then her own eyes, then their's, as CHALK stumbles around the

Get to Know your Duck

        room bumping into furniture and knocking things over as
        he coughs and wheezes)

TWINS
Visitor, visitor.

CONSTANCE
Don't look!

        (CHALK finally collapses onto the floor, passed out)

CONSTANCE
(Leaning over Chalk) Hello. Hello? I know who you are. You're that horrible man. My husband will be right back. (No response) Oh, my, you're quite a mess. (She brushes something off his shoulder. No response) Stay away from my children. (Cautiously she straightens him up against the wall. No response) I'm going to call the Sheriff. He'll be right over to take you away.

        (CONSTANCE combs CHALK's hair. No response. She
        replaces his hard hat. She backs away from him and picks
        up the phone, but is distracted by the mess he's made)

CONSTANCE (cont.)
Look what you've done to my living room.

        (She sets phone down and begins straitening things
        up. BELL rings in kitchen)

CONSTANCE
Dinner!

        (Forgetting Chalk, CONSTANCE EXITS to kitchen. Chalk
        wakens, looks around, sees Twins)

CHALK
What happened?

Get to Know your Duck

TWINS
Terrorist! Terrorist!

CHALK
Terrorist? I'll show you terror!

(CHALK stands and lurches toward TWINS)

TWINS
Radon! Radon! Sick him! Sick him!

RADON
Cough. Wheeze.

(KEY NOISE in front door)

CHALK
Now what?

(CHALK hides at far end of couch, still visible to audience. STEVEN ENTERS wearing gas mask which he removes along with his coat and hat, all of which somehow ends up on the floor)

STEVEN
I'm home.

TWINS
Trespasser. Trespasser.

STEVEN
Good kids. Taking care of mommy.

TWINS
Slurp. Slurp.

Get to Know your Duck

STEVEN

Not until after dinner.

TWINS

Ah, nuts. Ah, nuts.

(CONSTANCE looks in from kitchen)

CONSTANCE

Almost ready.

STEVEN

Did you see the sunset the weather department produced tonight? It was the prettiest hospital-green sunsets I've seen in weeks.

(STEVEN sits to read newspaper.)

STEVEN (cont.)

I could eat a cow.

TWINS

Moo, moo.

(The TV and all the lights go out)

CONSTANCE (From kitchen)

Not again!

TWINS

Daddy, daddy. Blind, blind.

STEVEN

No, no, you're not blind, it's just another little power outage. Perhaps a small nuclear plant meltdown. I'll go start the generator. Nothing to worry about.(TV and lights come back on) Now it's OK.

Get to Know your Duck

(STEVEN, who has stood up, sees CHALK and freezes. CHALK sees STEVEN and freezes)

STEVEN
Oh no!

CHALK
(Unable to speak or stand he reaches toward Steven) Cough, cough, hack, wheeze.

(CONSTANCE looks in from kitchen)

CONSTANCE
Oh! Watch out! That trespassing man is here! He made a mess.

STEVEN
Keep back! (He runs behind couch with the TWINS) Did you call the sheriff?

CONSTANCE
Uh, no, not exactly. Be careful!

STEVEN
(Frustrated with her) Dear...Never mind, stay in the kitchen. I'll call. (To Chalk) Keep back! (Cautiously he moves to phone, picks it up and dials) Hello.

CHALK
(Clutching his throat) Hello.

STEVEN
(Thinking he has someone on the phone) Is anyone there?

CHALK
It's me.

Get to Know your Duck

STEVEN
(Into phone) Sheriff?

CHALK
Chalk.

STEVEN
Who?

CHALK
(Into megaphone) Chalk. Professor Chalk.

STEVEN
(Realizing its Chalk) Oh, no! The phone's dead.

CHALK
The rest of us aren't far behind.

STEVEN
(Holding the phone like a club) You're not supposed to be here.

CHALK
I'm lucky to be anywhere. I should be dead.

STEVEN
The sheriff's looking for you.

CHALK
And the F.B.I. taps my phone, so what.

STEVEN
The sheriff knows you're here. He's coming to take you away so everything will be fine again.

Get to Know your Duck

CHALK
Fine! Fine! Everything's not fine! Nothing is fine and nothing's going to be fine! I'm dying, you're dying, we're all dying a long agonizing suffocation.(Pauses to catch his breath).

STEVEN
Sorry.

CHALK
Sorry!? That's it! We are in a sorry state, aren't we? Outside, the air's in a sorry state of smog contamination. My lungs are in a sorry state from extracting the few remaining particles of oxygen from the air. A horrible, sorry, choking mess.

STEVEN
Sorry.

CHALK
You used that answer---can't use it again. What else do you have to say?

STEVEN
I was warned about you.

CHALK
Everybody's been warned, but no one listens. (With MEGAPHONE) Stop consuming, stop polluting, stop the dirty corporate cavorting.

STEVEN
Who are you talking to?

CHALK
As always, only to myself.

STEVEN
Are you hard of hearing?

Get to Know your Duck

CHALK
I'm the only one left who still listens to me and even I don't like what I'm hearing. (Into megaphone) Mankind is a zit on mother earth's backside.

STEVEN
(Holding his ears) Ouch!

CHALK
You think that hurts? I'm hurt by the loss of forests and open fields. Do you remember open fields?

STEVEN
Open field?

CHALK
An outdoor space bigger than a parking lot.

STEVEN
Oh, yes, what ever happened...?

CHALK
Shopping malls and office complexes. Never mind. A little while ago, lost in the vile vapors, my gas-mask malfunctioned. I thought I was bedding down in the permanent worm bin. At least there I could do some good.

STEVEN
Worm bin?

CHALK
Yes, the one place left where I might be able to make a contribution to the earth.

STEVEN
I hope I'm not detecting a negative attitude.

CHALK
I hope I'm not detecting a daytime T.V attitude.

Get to Know your Duck

STEVEN
Say, I'm not supposed to be talking to you.

CHALK
Join the crowd.

STEVEN
I'm sorry, but, well, please go home.

CHALK
Yes, yes. Alright. I've been thrown out nuclear plants, toxic waste dumps, government offices (Searching in his pocket) Bambi? (Frantic) Bambi?! (He pulls a dead mouse from his pocket) Ah, Bambi, poor little girl. Oh, no...

STEVEN
What's that?

CHALK
Bambi. My little snookems. My pet mouse.

TWINS
Squeak, squeak.

CHALK
Poor baby, he must have been overwhelmed by the smog.

STEVEN
I'm sorry.

(STEVEN keeps his distance)
(CONSTANCE ENTERS)

CONSTANCE
Are we safe?

Get to Know your Duck

CHALK
(Excited) Safe? (Maniacal laugh) Safety is an illusion! (With MEGAPHONE, chanting) Doomed, doomed, dead as Bambi, we're all doomed.

CONSTANCE
(Frightened) Aaaaahhhh! He's going to kill us!

(CONSTANCE screams and runs around the room finally ending up in a protective posture near her children. CHALK and STEVEN watch in silent amazement)

CHALK
I don't know what people have told you about me, but I'm relatively harmless, not to mention ineffectual. I'd like to dispel the rumor that I eat babies. No, I'm an advocate for world peace, population control and environmental ecology. Retired faculty of State University, presently employed as a private consultant, lost in the smog and...(despondent) minus a best friend. (Holding out Bambi by the tail)

(CONSTANCE relaxes a bit)

CONSTANCE
(Disgusted, but moved) Yuck. Did she...have a family?

CHALK
Five generations. They'll be heartbroken.

CONSTANCE
Is there anything we can do?

TWINS
Ka-plop flush. Ka-plop flush.

CHALK
No, I'll take her home. There'll need to be a service and a wake...

Get to Know your Duck

STEVEN
Sorry. You know, you're only two blocks from your home. (Pointing to door) When you go out the door, just turn right...

CHALK
Strange, a few minutes ago I thought I was suffocating to death. Now here I am revived. I may yet live to die of cancer.

STEVEN
That's it! Look on the bright side.

CHALK
Of course. The world's a wonderful place, as long as we don't need to breath.

STEVEN
Yes, well, the air's thick, but...

CHALK
Thick! The air's thicker than it's ever been. I've measured it (he shows the gadget he's holding) as being 14 deciliter denser than it was during the big conversion two years ago.

STEVEN
If you say it's bad...

CHALK
The airs not bad, son, there isn't any air! Or, at least, not as much air as there are fumes and particles per million. Today I took readings around the pond.

STEVEN
Pond?

CHALK
Pond: "a body of water smaller than a lake."

Get to Know your Duck

STEVEN
Oh?

CHALK
It's that septic mess that folks now call 'the swamp'.

STEVEN
Oh, the swamp.

CHALK
Yes, it used to be called Clear Lake, years ago, then it was re-named Green Lake, then Black Lake and now it's just 'the swamp' because of Cow Chemical.

STEVEN
So! You were at the Cow factory! Out! Get out, you terrorist!

CHALK
Terrorist? I'm not a terrorist. I couldn't hurt a fly. I'm an ecologist.

STEVEN
Ecologist? Ha! You want to blow up Cow Chemical!

CHALK
Blow up...? I suppose the Sheriff told you that!

STEVEN
Yes, we're on to you and your...whiskers!

CHALK
Whiskers?

STEVEN
Yes, and ideas!

Get to Know your Duck

CHALK
Ideas? Yes, I plead guilty to ideas, but I'm for clean air and explosions contribute to air pollution.

CONSTANCE
Air? What's air got to do with anything?

CHALK
Gad, oxygen is what keeps us alive! No oxygen, no life, period. Oxygen, a colorless, odorless, gas.

STEVEN & CONSTANCE
Colorless and odorless?

CHALK
(Chalk looks at them as pitied imbeciles) Colored and flavored air is a fairly new invention, kids.

STEVEN
Oh.

CHALK
That's O2.

(CHALK takes out a piece of CHALK and writes O2 on the wall)

CONSTANCE
Ahhh! My wall.

CHALK
Air, in it's natural state, is made up of oxygen, nitrogen and small amounts of other gasses.

(CHALK writes a formula on the wall in chalk)

Get to Know your Duck

CONSTANCE

(Distressed) Ahh, ahh, ahh.

    (She takes out her desire to wipe off the wall by combing the Twins hair)

TWINS

Ouch. Ouch.

CHALK

Being invisible made it easier to see the mountains, the trees and even across the street.

STEVEN

Oh.

CHALK

Exactly, it may only be O by now. Very good, you're catching on.

    (CHALK writes O+ on the wall)

CONSTANCE

Oh, oh, oh.

CHALK

That's right, O-3, ozone. Very good, Constance. And now, Steven, what is this deadly stuff classified as?

STEVEN

Uhm…I'm sorry…I forgot.

CHALK

No, it's not "I forgot." You might try following Constance's example and do your reading, young man. O plus is a free radical.

STEVEN

Isn't that what you are?

Get to Know your Duck

CHALK
So, you're like the rest of them. You're against me too! Follow me, tap my phone, jam my computer! Read my e-mail! Why do I bother?

STEVEN
There's that attitude problem again.

CHALK
Attitude problem? Were you sent by the F.B.I. to turn my brain into mush?

CONSTANCE
Mush? Oh, dinner's ready.

(CHALK prepares to leave)

CHALK
Attitude! (Holding up Bambi by the tail) Bambi was not killed by a bad attitude! Goodbye. I'll just take my bad attitude and go home to my mice.

TWINS
Squeak, squeak.

CHALK
Yes, mice. I don't suppose it would make a dent in your gray matter if I told you I've been feeding swamp water to mice for ten generation and that each successive generation has greater degrees of malformation. What do you say to that!

(CONSTANCE and STEVEN are bewildered)

CHALK (cont.)
Exactly what I thought you'd say. And what's your response to the fact that some of my mice are born without tails, others without ears, many with erratic and stupid behavior, others with an inability to squeak and a few with a malicious attitude toward cheese!

Get to Know your Duck

(CONSTANCE and STEVEN shrug)

CHALK (cont.)
And your children are in the same boat. They're exposed to the same stinking mess of a world!

CONSTANCE
My children?

STEVEN
Your world may be a stinking mess, but ours is just fine.

(CHALK takes up the megaphone. Constance and Steven cringe. Chalk wilts.)

CHALK
Never mind.

(Silently, CHALK turns and EXITS.)

STEVEN
There's a man who never learned to put on a happy face.

CONSTANCE
(Holding her abdomen) My baby's going to be alright, isn't he?

STEVEN
Of course, he's going to be a healthy little squirt. Now, sure could sink my teeth into some food.

CONSTANCE
Uh, oh..(She starts to leave then hesitates). Speaking of teeth, Dear, I took ah...the twins to the dentist today and he says they really do need braces.

STEVEN
(Standing by Twins, he messes their hair) Oh no. What now?

Get to Know your Duck

CONSTANCE
He's very worried about their occlusions, which he described as being mal.

STEVEN
Oh? Gee, I never noticed any teeth sticking out crooked. Let's see.

> (He stands in front of the twins, who are only visible from behind by the audience, and goes through the motions of showing his teeth and bite)

STEVEN (cont)
Sally, Timmy, let dad see your teeth. Open wide. Good. Smile.

TWINS
Cheese. Cheese.

STEVEN
Close your teeth together. Go ahead, see if you can get a few more together. (To his wife) That's real close, Dear.

CONSTANCE
Doctor Carver says close doesn't make it, dear. He said he's been watching their teeth for two years hoping those spaces would fill in, but nature just didn't deal them a full deck -- teeth-wise.

STEVEN
Gee, I don't think they look so bad. How much will it cost?

CONSTANCE
Uhm, oh, $50,000.

STEVEN
$50,000! (He looks back to the twins) Open up. Now close. Harder. (He tries to push one twins mouth shut) Can't these gaps be filled with some kind of space-age material?

Get to Know your Duck

CONSTANCE
Uh... yes, the doctor mentioned a product that Cow Chemical, the chemist in our bathroom, is experimenting with.

STEVEN
Maybe I can pick up some samples. Why is it that every kid that walks into Carvers office comes out with a cyclone fence wrapped around his teeth?

CONSTANCE
Well, he said we could go straight to dentures, since they'll need them eventually anyway. I guess a lot of kids are getting them. Oh, I may be a little old fashioned, but I think if there is any chance at all we should try and keep the originals and braces.

>(CHALK ENTERS, rushing, wheezing. He carries a large barrel which he sets down)

CHALK
They're gone, they're gone...

TWINS
Visitor. Visitor.

>(CONSTANCE take up a defensive position near the TWINS. STEVEN has the phone)

STEVEN
What do you want? I'll call the sheriff.

CONSTANCE
Stay away! And don't leave that dirty barrel in here.

CHALK
They're gone. My mice, they're gone...gone...All my mice...

Get to Know your Duck

STEVEN
What are you talking about now?

CHALK
...all gone, Eli and Lilly, Proctor and Gamble, Oliver and North, Bill and Casey, Ronald and Nancy, Richard and Nixon...

STEVEN
How?

CONSTANCE
Who?

CHALK
Yes, all of them, even How and Who, all gone.

STEVEN
Who would steal mice?

CHALK
Oh no, Who was stolen, he wouldn't steal a Gorgonzola.

CONSTANCE
Why would he?

CHALK
No, no, Why actually hates cheese. Probably a symptom of a toxin effecting the brain...

CONSTANCE
What?

CHALK
Yes, What, too. All of them; Who, What, Why, When. Say, how do you know the names of my mice?

STEVEN
Why would anyone steal your mice?

Get to Know your Duck

CHALK
Elementary, or at the most middle school, they found out I was experimenting with their swamp water.

CONSTANCE
Who?

CHALK
No, Who was kidnaped. Cow Chemical. Cow Chemical owns the factory that spills the chemicals that fills the swamp that feeds the mice that develop the malformations.

STEVEN
Oh, no, now wait, a few mice decide to take the day off and ...

CHALK
(Despondent) It's over, first Bambi, now... no one listens...they beat me...my work...

STEVEN
They're probably hiding. A prank.

CHALK
They were in cages! My poor deformed little babies...my testimony...stole my mices...the legislature

STEVEN
Legislature?

CHALK
Legislature: a body of persons empowered to make, change or repeal laws.

STEVEN
Yes, but what does it have to do with your mice?

Get to Know your Duck

CHALK
Monday the legislature votes on the Gargantuan-fund for cleaning up the environment. I am scheduled to testify. To show them my experiments and prove that baby mice...

CONSTANCE
But, your poor little baby mice are gone.

CHALK
Yes, it's over. No testimony. No more mice...and they were so cute with their tiny flat feet...

CONSTANCE
Flat feet?

CHALK
Yes, and their funny little grins, because of the malocclusions.

CONSTANCE
Malocclusions?

CHALK
But, I'm not taking this lying down. This barrel's full of swamp water! I'm going to do what they said I was going to do---blow Cow Chemical to hell!

CONSTANCE & STEVEN
No!

TWINS
Fireworks! Fireworks!

CHALK
I just came by to warn you. Better clear out. (Short of breath) The swamp will ignite.

STEVEN
Professor, be reasonable.

Get to Know your Duck

CHALK
Reason! (In megaphone) There's no reason left.

TWINS
Too loud. Too loud.

CONSTANCE
But, Professor, is that what Bambi would have wanted?

CHALK
Bambi? Well, Bambi...Bambi was...

CONSTANCE
Was what?

CHALK
(Sheepishly) A committed pacifist. He followed the teachings of Gandhi.

STEVEN
You don't mean...

CHALK
Yes, he practiced passive resistance and shaved his head.

CONSTANCE
I'm sorry about your mice, Professor, but think about Bambi and the risk to others...

CHALK
Oh, you're right, but what can I do? I have nothing to go home to.

STEVEN
There's a basketball game on TV.

CHALK
There's no hope, is there?

Get to Know your Duck

CONSTANCE
I know, why don't you have dinner with us? You'll feel better after a hot meal. We're having chicken tetrazini T.V. dinners. Low sodium. And sterile with none of those messy life forms. For dessert we've got Cow Cream.

CHALK
I don't suppose it ever occurred to you that the list of ingredients in the chicken tetrazini and the so-called ice cream is the same?

CONSTANCE
(Proudly) The tetrazini has half the sugar and twice the artificial flavors.

CHALK
Shouldn't it be called Chicken Petrolzini?

CONSTANCE
And, it was on sale at the Cost-Cow store.

(KNOCK at door)

RADON
Cough, wheeze.

STEVEN
(To RADON) Down boy. (To CONSTANCE) Maybe it's the sheriff.

CHALK
(Alarmed) Sheriff? I'll show him who's a terrorist! That capitalist tool, that...

(CONSTANCE opens door and Mrs LEXIA ENTERS)

CONSTANCE
Mrs. Lexia. How are you.

Get to Know your Duck

TWINS
Visitor, visitor.

LEXIA
Well very. My kitten has a new little boy.

CONSTANCE
How sweet. I'll have to bring the twins over.

LEXIA
(Showing a LARGE CONTAINER) Do please. Borrow if I mind a gallon of sugar?

CONSTANCE
Oh, yes. I'll be right back.

(CONSTANCE EXITS to kitchen)

LEXIA
Hew-yew, Steven.

STEVEN
Hello, Mrs. Lexia.

LEXIA
You look like the weight of your shoulders is on the world.

STEVEN
Me? Never better.

(CONSTANCE ENTERS)

CHALK
How are you, Deserie?

LEXIA
(None friendly) Well very.

Get to Know your Duck

CHALK
I'm glad to hear that. Even if it is backwards.

(LEXIA ignores the comment. STEVEN and CONSTANCE are shocked)

CONSTANCE
Here you are.

LEXIA
A gallon of doctor a day keeps the sugar away.

CONSTANCE
Don't you say.

LEXIA
Do I always. Well, getting be best on.

STEVEN
Bye good.

LEXIA
Thank sugar for the you.

CONSTANCE
Welcome your.

(MRS. LEXIA EXITS)

STEVEN
(To Chalk) Do you Mrs. Lexia know?

CHALK
For thirty years. She was a friend of my late wife.

Get to Know your Duck

STEVEN
Not too friendly these days?

CHALK
People will give up almost anything, even old friends, to avoid the truth.

STEVEN
What do you mean?

CHALK
You noticed her solecism?

STEVEN
Was it showing?

CHALK
Solecism: "a violation of the conventional usage of language."

STEVEN
Well, yes.

CHALK
Did you ever say anything to her about it?

STEVEN
I didn't want to be impolite.

CHALK
No, certainly don't be impolite, just let yourself be poisoned into stupidity!

STEVEN
If you can't say anything nice, don't say anything at all.

CHALK
Why do I bother?

Get to Know your Duck

CONSTANCE
What's wrong with Mrs. Lexia?

CHALK
Five years ago, after it had been going on for about six months, I pointed out that her problem might be a consequence of her use of a common mind-altering drug.

CONSTANCE
Mrs. Lexia takes drugs?

CHALK
Yes. Extracted, concentrated and crystallize from natural sources and poured into the blood stream to promote a sense of well-being.

STEVEN
Cocaine?

CHALK
Sugar. I merely suggested she go off sugar for few weeks to test my theory.

STEVEN
She didn't agree?

CHALK
She became quite angry and said there was nothing speech with her wrong.

CONSTANCE
You're against sugar?

TWINS
Kill him. Kill him.

CHALK
The Twins are right! Kill the messenger.

Get to Know your Duck

CONSTANCE
Now, now, everyone pull up a TV tray. Perhaps a good dinner will cheer you up?

(CONSTANCE EXITS to kitchen)

STEVEN
(Setting up TV trays (and making a mess) Nothing fancy. We're a meat and potatoes and T.V. kind of family.

CHALK
Kids watch too much TV. Their brains get zapped with cathode rays, filled with commercials to buy, buy, buy.

TWINS
Buy sugar, buy sugar.

CHALK
Certainly, buy sugar, buy preservatives, buy plastic...

(CONSTANCE enters with FOOD and serves everyone including the TWINS who remain on the couch. After setting out the twins food she picks up the EGG)

CONSTANCE
I'll just throw this filthy egg out.

CHALK
What's that?!

CONSTANCE
Just an old egg the Twins found in the swamp today.

CHALK
Is it alive?

CONSTANCE
No, I don't think so. I didn't see it move.

Get to Know your Duck

CHALK
May I see?

STEVEN
There's nothing the matter is there?

CHALK
This is the first sighting of nesting in the swamp in years. What in the name of Darwin is this? It's too big to be a duck or goose...(He puts his ear against the egg shell. The audience hears a heart beat)...(softly, then louder) it's alive...it's alive...Steven, Constance, listen, we may have life here!

>(STEVEN and CONSTANCE lean over the egg and listen. The heartbeat is heard by the audience)

CONSTANCE
Do I hear a noise?

CHALK
(Laughing) You hear more than noise, dear Constance. You hear the basic rhythm of life. (He starts drumming to the heart beat) Hear it? Hear the beat? Hear that crazy beat? Dig it kids, that's syncopation. That's rhythm. That's the music of life.

>(STEVEN and CONSTANCE watch as CHALK does a little dance)

STEVEN
The bathroom's down the hall...

CHALK
Don't you two get it? It's a heart. (Hitting his chest in time with) It pumps blood. It keeps us alive and inside this egg there's one beating out the message. I'm alive, I'm alive, I'm alive.

Get to Know your Duck

TWINS

Lub-dub. Lub-dub.

CONSTANCE

Alive? Like a baby?

CHALK

Yes! Just like a human baby, this egg has the potential to hatch and be born.

CONSTANCE

And stain the carpet?

TWINS

Croak, croak.

STEVEN

Don't tease your mother.

CONSTANCE

(Softly) Steven, there's a baby in the egg! Isn't that exciting?

STEVEN

A bird? Not another canary.

CHALK

(Standing, holding the egg, his enthusiasm turns to pessimism) This poor bird...soon it will be part of this dreadful world.

STEVEN

Don't miscount your chickens before they're hatched.

CONSTANCE

Come on, Professor, have something to eat. It'll help.

(Constance and Steven sit to eat. Steven makes a mess)

Get to Know your Duck

CHALK
(Lost in thought) Do you mind if I keep this egg? Perhaps I can do something with it. I was a professor of biology.

STEVEN & CONSTANCE
(Eating) Mmmm.

CHALK
I loved teaching, back when students were able to read and write. There is nothing like the fascination on a young person's face when he looks inside his first dissected frog.

TWINS
Croak, croak.

STEVEN
It's not funny.

CHALK
Its little green legs pinned down, its tongue hanging out, as if to say, explore me, find my pink heart, my red stomach, my yellow brain...
    (STEVEN and CONSTANCE slow their eating)

CONSTANCE
Uh.

CHALK
But, I had higher ambitions. It's fine to teach a child to cut open a frog and pull out a string of slimy entrails.

(STEVEN & CONSTANCE do not look well)

Get to Know your Duck

CHALK cont.
But I felt it wasn't enough, I was tainted with a disease that made me care. I knew the world was turning into a putrid, vile, latrine, that the excrement of society, the waste of consumerism, was backing up and suffocating us.

CONSTANCE
How about a cold glass of cow-juice, Professor?

CHALK
No thanks. This heavy smog has upset my digestion and makes me feel like vomiting.

(CONSTANCE & STEVEN are just looking at their food now)

CHALK (cont.)
So I left the university and dedicated myself to teaching on a larger scale through environmental political activism. I traded the squishy guts of the frog for the spongy gray matter of mankind's brain.

STEVEN
(Staring into his half-eaten dinner and looking ill) Ooooo.

CHALK
And what good did it do me? My views have not made me popular.

STEVEN
You've made me sick.

(STEVEN gags and runs, EXITING to kitchen)

CHALK
See what I mean?

CONSTANCE
Well, you have other qualities...

Get to Know your Duck

CHALK

No, I know I'm opinionated, verbose, disagreeable...

STEVEN

(In kitchen doorway) And nauseating.

CHALK

I thought I was right, always right, and that I was doing some good, that someday people would listen to me. Until today...

CONSTANCE

I keep thinking of poor little Bambi.

TWINS

Croak. Croak.

STEVEN

(To TWINS) Don't tease the professor. (TO CHALK) You know, I have a tape you might be interested in. It's called, Let a Smile Be Your Umbrella

CHALK

(Wheezing) Does it work for acid rain? Can't I make you see? Is my whole life a waste? Don't you understand, this is big, catastrophic, your future, your children.

CONSTANCE

My children?

CHALK

Yes! Your children! Future children! My mice proved the connection between pollution and children and the dentist.

CONSTANCE

This has something to do with my children?

STEVEN

If there's a problem, tell the authorities.

Get to Know your Duck

CHALK
Publicity takes money. Our last fund-raising event...(Wheeze) the Ralph Nader look-alike contest...(he goes into a coughing fit, gasps and slumps back exhausted)

CONSTANCE
Take it easy professor, we're on your side.

STEVEN
Dear...

CHALK
Are you? Complacency is Cow Chemical's best friend.

CONSTANCE
Cow Chemical, the chemist in our classrooms?

STEVEN
Cow Chemical? What do they have to...

CHALK
Cow Chemical, the chemist of our swamp.

STEVEN
What do you mean, swamp?

CHALK
Swamp. A tract of wet, spongy land.

STEVEN
Excuse me, Professor, you keep complaining about the swamp, but Dr. Golf says that the swamp has never hurt anyone and he's been the town doctor for years and he ought to know.

Get to Know your Duck

CHALK
(Excited) Dr. Golf! Dr. Golf! That Quack! That tonsil puller! That eardrum poker! Why, he doesn't know anything about health. He never took a class in Environmental Medicine.

STEVEN
He has a degree in Family Medicine.

CHALK
Right, but not your family. His family is the Cow Chemical Company, chemist to our medical schools. That pill-pusher Golf was trained by the pill makers. They have no interest in preventive medicine.

> (CONSTANCE picks up EGG during Chalk's diatribe and examines it, holding it gently, like a baby)

STEVEN
Surely the doctor would know if all those chemical 'pollutants', as you call them, were harmful.

CHALK
And what are his medicines made of? The Cow Chemical Company manufactures drugs out of the same vats of chemicals they use to make pesticides and vinyl siding.

STEVEN
And they do a great job. You see, I...

CHALK
For Dr. Golf to look too judiciously at chemical poisoning he would have to seriously question his own work, his livelihood, the foundation of his life.

STEVEN
Professor, excuse me, but chemicals are our friends.

Get to Know your Duck

CHALK
Not petro-chemicals. Why do you think the air smells like plastic?

STEVEN
Well, what about the automobile? Without petro-chemicals...

CHALK
Nonsense. Henry Ford build an automobile out a soybean plastic and powered it with ethanol in 1941! (Chalk sputters into a coughing fit)

CONSTANCE
(Caressing the egg) Steven, perhaps we should...(signaling toward bedroom)...you know.

STEVEN
(To Constance) Oh, yes. (To Chalk) Constance always take the twins to Dr. Golf when they're sick.

CHALK
My point exactly. He's got no orientation toward health, only disease. He was trained for direct military confrontation. Why do you think his boss is called The Surgeon General?

STEVEN
Professor, this is just the way the world works, it's part of living in the 21st century, it's part of natural selection. And natural selection is, well, natural.

> (CONSTANCE sets EGG down and EXITS to bedroom making signals to Steven)

CHALK
The duck is the agent of natural selection for the slug. The slug has no choice, but has adapted well enough over thousands of years. I've been trying to get people to exercise choice, but they'd rather be selected for extermination by a C.E.O.

> (CONSTANCE ENTERS carrying a tray full of prescription bottles)

Get to Know your Duck

CONSTANCE
(TO STEVEN) My, my look at the time. Here, dear, here's your medicine. Remember our squirt project.

STEVEN
Yes. Alright.

CHALK
(Using MEGAPHONE he startles Steven and Constance) Look at the swamp, look at the sky, look at that jumbo egg sitting there. The first egg in years, maybe our last, and we don't even know what it's going to be.

STEVEN
I'm sorry, Cow Chemical has been very good to me and my family. I trust them. Professor, I'm just an average guy, I just want to raise my family and be left alone.

CHALK
Left alone? Slime mold is crawling down the walls of your house. You call that alone?

CONSTANCE
Oh, I try to keep my house clean. I use my Scum-Buster and Smog-O-Matic.

STEVEN
And you do a great job, honey.
    (CONSTANCE takes a modified blowtorch from the closet and blasts away at the mold on the wall)

CONSTANCE
I scour and boil every day.

STEVEN
Everything will be fine in the morning. A good night's sleep. A new day...

Get to Know your Duck

CONSTANCE
(TO STEVEN) Yes! (signals toward the bedroom) Why don't we take our pills and go to bed.

CHALK
What about my mice with malocclusions?

CONSTANCE
(Hysterical) That's what we have dentists for!

STEVEN
(To Constance) Dear...(To Chalk) Wasn't that in a laboratory and with rodents.

TWINS
Squeak, squeak.

CONSTANCE
Oh, it's bedtime, uhm, Huston and John. (STEVEN looks at her, worried) I have got to get them to bed. Pills, my pills (She begins frantically popping lids off the pill bottles) One to sleep, one for the morning headache...

CHALK
No! No! You can't do this to yourselves!

> (As CHALK stands he stumbles and knocks the tray from her, the pills fly)

STEVEN
Ooops.

CONSTANCE
Ahhhh!

CHALK
No! Forgive me...

Get to Know your Duck

CONSTANCE
(Hysterical) My pills, my pills...

STEVEN
I hate to say it, but see where anger leads you?

CHALK
(Admonishing himself) You old fool! You've done it again.

CONSTANCE
Look at this mess!

    (CONSTANCE grabs vacuum cleaner and vacuums pills)

STEVEN
Nothing's broken. Everything will be fine.

CHALK
Fine!? (Suddenly weak) Fine. Never mind, I'll go. (Picks up egg) Come on, little fella.

TWINS
Smog. Smog.

    (CHALK goes to front door and opens it. A cloud of smog rushes in and envelopes him. He's sent into a coughing and wheezing attack that throws him back into the room. He loses control of the egg and it flies into the air)

CONSTANCE
Steven!

    (STEVEN catches EGG, sets it down and catches CHALK)

CONSTANCE (cont.)
Oh, good! Egg is so hard to clean up.

Get to Know your Duck

(CONSTANCE blows the smog back outside. STEVEN takes CHALK to the chair)

CHALK
Let me go. (COUGH, WHEEZE)

RADON
Cough, wheeze.

(STEVEN sits CHALK in chair. CHALK is barely conscious)

STEVEN
(To Chalk) You see how Constance worked the Smog-O-Matic?

TWINS
Varoom. Varoom.

CONSTANCE
Thank you, dear.

STEVEN
That's made by Cow Electric, our subsidiary. You can blow it, you can vac it. Even has a wet-vac setting for that extra wet smog.

CONSTANCE
And it takes smog spots off the windows.

STEVEN
See? Life is good, not perfect, maybe, not always clear, maybe. I like to have all my facts orderly.

CHALK
(Very weak) I'm just afraid that by the time things are clear, by the time all our facts are orderly, we'll all have malocclusions, flat feet, two heads, four eyes...

Get to Know your Duck

(CHALK drifts off to sleep. CONSTANCE combs his hair)

STEVEN
He's asleep. The poor old deranged madman.

CONSTANCE
Yes. You do think he really is deranged?

STEVEN
Of course. Who else would believe such nonsense about the world? A pessimist. A negative thinker.

CONSTANCE
He seems so certain. I worry about the kids---and his mice being stolen...

STEVEN
Not necessarily stolen. Perhaps they were looking for a more positive environment. And the twins are fine.

TWINS
Frogs. Frogs. Frogs. Frogs.

STEVEN
Don't tease your mother.

CONSTANCE
I guess you're right. (Looking at her watch (and wiping it) Oh my, midnight. We only have ten hours to get the specimen. Bedtime kids.

TWINS
Nightmares. Nightmares.

STEVEN
We'll tuck you in.

Get to Know your Duck

CHALK
(Snoring)

>(As lights fade, Steven picks up Twins and carries them off)

TWINS
Chant to us? Chant to us?

CONSTANCE
My uterus is round. My tubes are open. My ovum is fertile...

>(STEVEN, CONSTANCE and TWINS EXIT)
>(Lights out)

ACT I, Scene 3

>(In the dark, CHALK's snoring becomes louder. LIGHTS up to reveal CHALK sleeping in chair. After a few moment a loud cracking noise wakes CHALK)

CHALK
(Waking) Holy Darwin, who's there? (CHALK turns on the floor lamp, rises and goes to egg) Bless my chromosomes, what do we have here? Can you make it out little fellah? So, you're going to live. Life, zippity-do life! Prove me wrong, come on, prove me wrong. (With MEGAPHONE) Steven, Constance, we've got a live one here!

>(Light comes on in the bedroom)

CHALK (cont.)
I don't know what it is yet, but it's alive.

Get to Know your Duck

(STEVEN and CONSTANCE ENTER)

STEVEN
Nothing's the matter, is it?

CONSTANCE
Children? Where are my children?

CHALK
Your children are fine. Look here. Look, it's hatching!
It looks like it's time for the new addition to our community.

CONSTANCE & STEVEN
Ahhh?

CHALK
You're welcome. I knew you wouldn't want to miss this. Better get the Twins up.

(STEVEN and CONSTANCE shuffle over to the egg)

CONSTANCE
Did it break?

CHALK
No, it's cracking. Cracking open from the inside. The emergence of life.

STEVEN
Life?

CHALK
Yes, as opposed to death. Animate as opposed to inanimate. Capable of metabolism, reproduction, adaptation to the environment...

Get to Know your Duck

CONSTANCE
And staining the carpet?

STEVEN
Didn't I say so, Professor, life is good.

CONSTANCE
Look, we're going to have the patter of little feet around the house.

(ALL move in close around the egg)

CHALK
Maybe flat feet.

CONSTANCE
Flat feet?

STEVEN
Does that mean I have to pay for more orthotics?

CHALK
Webbed feet. It is alive, but...what's that color? Is that fur or feathers?

STEVEN
Ooo, it's ugly.

CONSTANCE
Oh, it's such a mess!

(CONSTANCE and STEVEN move away)

STEVEN
We don't have to watch this, dear. Oh, no. It's grotesque, covered in slime!

Get to Know your Duck

CHALK
Newborns of all species are often ugly; it's a form of self-defense that only parents can defend against. Humans have even extended that ugly period into puberty.

CONSTANCE
Professor, what kind of baby is it?

CHALK
Well, folks, it's definitely a...a...a duck. (Dramatic music)

STEVEN & CONSTANCE
A duck?. (Dramatic music)

(CONSTANCE and STEVEN move closer)

CHALK
Yes, a duck. (They pause and look around for the dramatic music which doesn't happen) But, there are two aspects which bother me. One is the size, it is simply too big for a new-born duck, it looks more to be four of five weeks old.

STEVEN
Please, I don't want to hear any more.

(STEVEN and CONSTANCE move away)

CHALK
The second problem is that the anatomy is not quite right, there is a distinctive anatomical flaw. (Dramatic music)

CONSTANCE & STEVEN
A flaw? (Dramatic music)

(STEVEN and CONSTANCE move closer to the egg)

Get to Know your Duck

CHALK
Yes, a flaw. (They wait in vain for the Dramatic music)

STEVEN & CONSTANCE
What's the flaw?

CHALK
This duck has two heads! (Dramatic music)

STEVEN & CONSTANCE
Two heads? (Dramatic music)

(STEVEN and CONSTANCE move back again)

CHALK
Yes, two heads.

(They look, again in vain, for the Dramatic music)

CONSTANCE
Do you mean twins, professor? Another set of twins in the Bland household?

CHALK
No, Constance, one duck, two heads, four eyes.

STEVEN
Good God!

CHALK
No, bad genes.

CONSTANCE
(meekly) Oh, is that rare?

Get to Know your Duck

CHALK
Rare to the point of being un-done. Rare, scarce, uncommon, unique. A proverbial freak.

STEVEN
A freak?

CHALK
Yes, "a sudden and apparently causeless turn of events, any abnormal or curiously unusual person or animal."

(CHALK reaches in to pick up the newborn bird.)

CONSTANCE & STEVEN
Watch out, Professor!   Professor, be careful!

CHALK
(Startled, he jumps back, grabs his heart)
What's the matter!?

STEVEN
It may attack!

CHALK
Horsefeathers! (He gently picks up the duckling) Don't you see, this duck is defenseless. We assaulted this bird when it was only an undeveloped egg in it's mothers womb and a glimmer in his fathers eye.

STEVEN
What do you mean we? I...

CHALK
We, as in you and I and them (points to the audience)

(CONSTANCE, seeing audience, makes sure her robe is closed. STEVEN, seeing audience, circles his ear with his finger to indicate that he thinks Chalk is crazy)

Get to Know your Duck

CHALK
We assaulted its parents with plastic holders from six-packs of beer and Styrofoam containers from fast-food restaurants. We poisoned its parents and grandparents with DDT and PCB's and M&Ms.

CONSTANCE
Pollution? Are you saying pollution did this to this baby?

CHALK
This bird didn't get this way by thinking bad thoughts. Don't worry, his bird can't do more than peck our toes and poop on your lawn. But we shat on his genes.

(CONSTANCE and STEVEN move closer)

CONSTANCE
Oh, look at his mouth!

STEVEN
No, don't look!

CHALK
(Solemnly) Yes, malocclusions.

CONSTANCE
Come to think of it, all the twins friends have things wrong; irregular teeth, feet with fallen arches...

STEVEN
But only little things...

CONSTANCE
Welts and rashes...

STEVEN
A few superficial problems...

Get to Know your Duck

CONSTANCE
Some of them are giants. Their glands rage out of control, hormones seep through their pores...and stain the furniture.

STEVEN
That's normal...

CONSTANCE
Steven, kids never used to have gland problems.

STEVEN
Glands? I never had glands.

CHALK
Have you considered it may be their environment?

CONSTANCE
I hadn't thought of it, but...They're either hyperactive, or want to be. Half of them are classified as slow learners, dyslexics, or behavior problems.

STEVEN
Look at the bright side, at least there's not anything seriously wrong with them. They're not blind like the Smiths or deaf like the Jones or dead like the Johnsons.

CONSTANCE
Steven, what about my memory?

CHALK
Memory is always one of the first things to fail...

STEVEN
There's nothing wrong. Well, they're only words...Anyone can forget a word here or there...

CONSTANCE
My children's names! Steven, look at this poor baby.

Get to Know your Duck

STEVEN
It's...cute. Twice as cute. Just like the twins.

CONSTANCE
(Holding her belly) And sterility! Half the couples we know sleep with specimen containers.

STEVEN
See, science is providing an answer. Everything's going to be alright as long as we have a reliable source of specimen containers.

CONSTANCE
(Pleading) Steven.

STEVEN
And those specimen containers are made, I might add, by Cow Chemical.

CONSTANCE
Professor, do you think it's too late for us? Do you think we can still have teeth and arches and babies?

>(CHALK holding the duckling {a hand-puppet} which is starting to move around and make noises. CHALK wearily sits down on a nearby chair)

CHALK
I don't know. I've been talking, writing letters and carrying protest signs about Cow Chemical for years, but this takes my wind away.

STEVEN
Cow Chemical? Cow Chemical is not the problem, it's the solution.

CHALK
My mice drinking massive amounts of pond water over several generations and developing oddities, that I expected, but this duck, something in the wild being so deformed by Cow Chemical...

Get to Know your Duck

STEVEN
No, not Cow Chemical. I'm sorry, I can't listen, I can't hear you.

(Steven covers his ears)

CHALK
Nobody listens! Gad, I'm exhausted. All the lead I've been breathing seems to have pooled in my feet.

CONSTANCE
What about future ducklings? What about dogs and cats and chickens and, and...babies?

CHALK
What can I do? (Referring to STEVEN) Look, no one listens to me.

STEVEN
(Still covering his ears) Are you saying something? I don't hear you.

CONSTANCE
Professor, I'm listening.

CHALK
You are?

DUCK
Quack. Quack.

CONSTANCE
Yes. What's going to happen to my children?

CHALK
You...I... (choked up) You heard what I said?

STEVEN
(Having heard) I hear nothing.

Get to Know your Duck

CONSTANCE
Yes, I hear. What can we do?

DUCK
Quack. Quack.

RADON
Cough, wheeze.

CHALK
Do? Well...I, you see...No body's ever asked me that. Do?

CONSTANCE
Yes. Is there something we can do to protect my babies?

(STEVEN puts his hands over CONSTANCE'S ears)

STEVEN
Don't listen to him. He's anti-Cow.

DUCK
Quack. Quack.

TWINS (OS)
(From their bedroom) Duck, duck. Duck, duck.

STEVEN
The Twins are awake! See what's happened...

CONSTANCE
(Pulling away from STEVEN) They're alright. Steven, please, I want to hear what the professor has to say.

CHALK
(A pronouncement) Cow Chemical has been secretly dumping chemicals into the pond...

Get to Know your Duck

STEVEN
I won't let my children hear this! I'm leaving.

(STEVEN walks to door)

CHALK
I snuck down to the factory and was trying to catch them tonight.

STEVEN
(Standing in doorway) Constance, our children need us.

(CONSTANCE stands and holds out a hand to STEVEN. Lights slow fade except for spot on STEVEN standing in open door)

CONSTANCE
Steven, won't you stay with me and listen.

STEVEN
N...N... I'm checking on the Twins.

CONSTANCE
But they're fine...

STEVEN
And, tomorrow's another work day. Good night.

(STEVEN EXITS. Lights on CHALK and CONSTANCE fade to black leaving room dark except for spot on closed door)

DUCK
Quack. Quack.

Get to Know your Duck

RADON
Cough, wheeze.

DUCK
Quack, quack.

(etc. as)

(SPOT FADES TO BLACK)

(End of Act I)

ACT II, SCENE 1

(The next morning. The Bland living room. The slime on the wall, which had been cleaned off the night before, has returned. There is also a slime growing on the windows. The TWINS are sitting on the couch. The DUCK, in a large box, cannot be seen except for portions of his wings now and again. CONSTANCE is sitting in chair reading. A large stack of books is on the ironing board. STEVEN ENTERS, appearing at the hallway door still in his pajamas)

STEVEN
(Looking sheepish, he CLEARS HIS THROAT)

CONSTANCE
(Not looking up from book) Good morning.

Get to Know your Duck

STEVEN
(His voice cracking) Constance?

(CONSTANCE slowly, unsmiling, turns toward him. She looks as if she's been crying)

CONSTANCE
(She SNIFFLES and wipes her eyes)

(With shit-eating grin, STEVEN hold up a full gallon container full of liquid)

STEVEN
Have I got a squirt-and-a-half for you.

(CONSTANCE runs to him)

CONSTANCE
(SOBBING) Oh, Stevey.

(They embrace. STEVEN spills some of SPECIMEN)

STEVEN
Opsy. Sorry about the carpet.

CONSTANCE
Never mind the carpet. It'll live. Steven, I don't know if I can go through with the squirt.

STEVEN
What do you mean?

CONSTANCE
Professor Chalk lent me some books. I've been reading...

Get to Know your Duck

STEVEN
(Fearful) Reading what?

CONSTANCE
About endangered species.

STEVEN
Why would you want to spoil your whole day?

CONSTANCE
(Weepy) It's so sad.

STEVEN
This could have been a fine day. A safe home, a loving family, a gallon of squirt...

>(CHALK, who has been lying, unseen, in a stuffed chair, sits up)

CHALK
(Standing, weakly) Oh, sure, the air is a septic mess, my life's work stolen, my little Bambi dead---a fine day.

>(CHALK, exhausted by his outburst, flops back into chair. CONSTANCE sits on the chair's arm and puts her arm around CHALK and combs his hair)

CONSTANCE
I'm so sorry about your little mice.

>(CONSTANCE, uncomfortable, looks and finds she is sitting on a larger than normal duck feather. She pulls it out and begins unconsciously letting it slowly swing back and forth in front of them)

Get to Know your Duck

STEVEN
Dear, don't you think you'd feel better if you went to see Dr. Golf and the nurse?

CONSTANCE
Professor Chalk and I talked late into the night.

STEVEN
It's unhealthy to go without sleep.

CONSTANCE
I want to do something to help.

CHALK
You do?

CONSTANCE
You know what they say; two heads are better than one.

>   (Two heads of DUCK, considerably grown, look out from box)

STEVEN
(Dejected) Oh.

CONSTANCE
If there's really a connection between the mice and the swamp...

STEVEN
(Covering his ears) Must this day be soiled?

TWINS
Croak. Croak.

STEVEN
It's not funny.

Get to Know your Duck

CONSTANCE
(Holding up the large feather) Steven, look.

CHALK
Help? Goodness, this changes everything.

STEVEN
(Seeing the feather, he moves his hands from his ears to his eyes) Don't try and confuse me with facts.

CHALK
(Lost in thought) Those little mices were my family. Their pathetic attempts to eat with those malocclusions, the blind ones bumping into each other, the extra legs, the languid behavior, the teenager's propensity to join gangs, the high rate of divorce, sure they had their problems, but they were family. Pity, all the males were sterile....

CONSTANCE
(Whimpering) Oh? Sterile? Steven? Did you hear that? The mice had no squirt.

STEVEN
There's nothing wrong with me.

CONSTANCE
Oh, Steven, this isn't about your squirt.

CHALK
Oh, it might be. My male mice had itty-bitty...

CONSTANCE
Professor Chalk can use the duck to prove the swamp water causes deformities.

Get to Know your Duck

STEVEN
(Pacing nervously) Am I having a bad dream? What is all this about? (Stopping in front of the box, he turns and faces Chalk and Constance) So what if there's a duck with a little problem...

(DUCK head emerges from box and looks STEVEN in the eye)

DUCK
Quack.

STEVEN
A slight flaw...

(The other DUCK head, behind STEVEN, emerges)

DUCK
Quack.

STEVEN
(Turning to see second head) A minor anomaly.

CONSTANCE
Anomaly?

CHALK
Anomaly. An unusual feature or characteristic...

CONSTANCE
Steven!

STEVEN
Truth is stranger than fiction.

CONSTANCE
But this is science fiction!

Get to Know your Duck

(Steven turns back and forth between the two heads of the duck alternately covering his eyes and ears as each head quacks at him)

DUCK

Quack...Quack...Quack (etc.)

(The Twins join in)

TWINS

Duck, duck, duck, duck...(etc.)

STEVEN

So, it's a little big...

CHALK

Ten times normal, twenty-four hours after birth. It's a big quacker.

DUCK

Quack, quack.

TWINS

Too big. Too big.

CONSTANCE

Mommy loves you, Timmy and Sally. (Combing their hair)

(Constance and Steven note she's gotten the names right)

DUCK

(More aggressively) Quack, quack, quack, quack, quack.

CONSTANCE

(Combing Duck's head feathers) Do you think something's wrong with him?

Get to Know your Duck

TWINS
Slugs. Slugs.

CONSTANCE
Yes, he must be hungry and thirsty.

CHALK
Brilliant deduction. Here...

>(CHALK grabs container of semen from STEVEN who tries to hold it, but loses his grip.

STEVEN
Wait!

>(CHALK holds container for DUCK who quickly slurps it down)

STEVEN & CONSTANCE
Ahhhh.....

>(DUCK is very happy and kisses each of them)

STEVEN   CONSTANCE
Yuck. Blah. Yuck.   I'm sick.

CONSTANCE
(Sorry at the loss of semen) Darling...

STEVEN
(Referring to container) I held it as long as I could...

Get to Know your Duck

CHALK
So, that's what duck's breath smells like. Well, he seems to be a friendly creature, if not altogether size/species proportional.
(Petting DUCK and messing it's feathers) Weren't you two on your way out?

CONSTANCE
No, I'd changed my mind, anyway.

STEVEN
(Struck) So, you don't want to have another child?

>(CONSTANCE and STEVEN turn and look at each other, frozen)

CONSTANCE
No, not for ever...just for now, until we know more.

CHALK
(TO DUCK) Would you be willing to testify before Congress about a certain swamp?

DUCK
Quack. Quack.

TWINS
Swamp. Swamp.

STEVEN
OK, Constance, if it means that much to you, go ahead, see what you can do about finding out if there's a connection between the swamp and the...little problems. Meanwhile, I'm going to work.

CONSTANCE
Alright.

Get to Know your Duck

CHALK
Oh, Steven, before you go, could you help an old man carry this poor little fella into the garage? I'd like to perform some tests on him.

STEVEN
Well, sure.

(STEVEN and CHALK EXIT carrying the box out through the kitchen with effort)

(The DOORBELL rings)

CONSTANCE
Oh, now what?

RADON
Cough, wheeze.

CONSTANCE
(Opening the door) Uh, daddy!

TWINS
Oink, oink.

CONSTANCE
Keep reading Sally and Timmy.

(SHERIFF ENTERS, uninvited)

CONSTANCE (cont.)
Come in.

SHERIFF
I see that I am.

(Awkward silence as SHERIFF looks around)

Get to Know your Duck

CONSTANCE
What can I do for you?

SHERIFF
Where's Steven?

CONSTANCE
In the garage. Do you want to see him?

SHERIFF
I see that I do.

CONSTANCE
I'll be right back.

SHERIFF
See that you are.

(CONSTANCE goes to the window, opens it, knocks away several stalactites of green slime which are hanging from the window sill)

CONSTANCE
Steven, Daddy's here, could you come in? He wants to speak with you.

(Awkward silence as CONSTANCE waits with SHERIFF)

CONSTANCE
What have you been up to?

SHERIFF
Fishin'.

CONSTANCE
Catch any?

Get to Know your Duck

SHERIFF

Limited.

CONSTANCE

I see that you are.

    (SHERIFF is not sure of her meaning)
    (STEVEN ENTERS through kitchen)

STEVEN

Mornin', Sheriff. Up awfully early aren't you?

SHERIFF

You got a problem with that?

STEVEN

Sorry.

SHERIFF

I'm still looking for Professor Chalk. Thought you might have seen him.

STEVEN

Oh, well, that's right, the phone was out...

TWINS

Squeak, squeak.

CONSTANCE

(Realizing the connection) Maybe the professor's home with his mice?

    (SHERIFF, surprised by the comment, looks at
    CONSTANCE askance)

SHERIFF

(To Steven) I'm busy. Have you seen the old degenerate?

Get to Know your Duck

STEVEN
Sorry. Yes. Say, did you hear about the mice...?

SHERIFF
(Nervously) What mice?

STEVEN
Chalk's mice, the ones in cages with tails and whiskers.

SHERIFF
A rumor. Publicity stunt. No mice. Never was. OK, where's Chalk?

>(CONSTANCE and STEVEN shocked at SHERIFF's answer)

STEVEN
(Confused) Ah, well, he's...

CONSTANCE
Dear, isn't it time for you to be at work?

STEVEN
Gosh, yes, I better get going. (To Sheriff) Chalk's...

CONSTANCE
Steven!

STEVEN
What? (Realizing what Constance wants) Oh. Sheriff, Chalk's not as bad as he might seem.

SHERIFF
Oh, cat poop! Is he here?

STEVEN
N...N...N, Yes.

Get to Know your Duck

SHERIFF
Where?!

STEVEN
In the garage.

CONSTANCE
Steven!

STEVEN
I can't tell a lie.

CONSTANCE
Daddy, did it ever occur to you that I might have seen Professor Chalk and that I might even know where he is and even be able to tell you where he is without the aid of my husband?

SHERIFF
No.

(CHALK ENTERS from kitchen. Angry, CONSTANCE EXITS to kitchen)

CHALK
I took a sample of the duck's genes...

SHERIFF
What?

CHALK
(Chilly) Good day, sheriff.

SHERIFF
Chalk, I've been looking for you.

CHALK
And you found me, remarkable.

Get to Know your Duck

SHERIFF
What's going on around here. (Reading books on table) The Big Book of Ducks, The Duck Stops Here, Amphibians That Quack, The Readers Digest Condensed Duck, Raising Ducks for Fun and Profit, How to Train Your Duck to do Tricks...

TWINS
Quack, quack, quack, quack.

SHERIFF
Did you say something about a ducks britches when you come in, Chalk?

CHALK
Britches?

SHERIFF
Yea, you said something about duck pants.

CHALK
Pants?

SHERIFF
Don't deny it, you said duck jeans.

CHALK
Oh, genes...why, yes, I guess I did.

SHERIFF
Duck jeans?

CHALK
Yes, by taking a tissue sample, extracting the DNA molecule...

SHERIFF
DNA? DNA!? Isn't that...

Get to Know your Duck

CHALK

A double helix?

SHERIFF

...pro-life?

CHALK

Indubitably.

(CONSTANCE ENTERS)

SHERIFF

Oh, cow pies! Ducks in pants! Chalk, I'm arresting you!

CHALK

Oh yea!

CONSTANCE

What!? Why?

SHERIFF

For trespassing at Cow Chemical.

CHALK

Ha! Civil disobedience! (He slumps to floor) My favorite exercise! You'll have to carry me out.

SHERIFF

Don't be a big sissy. Stand up and go to jail like a man.

(During the next several exchanges, SHERIFF attempts to pull the slumping CHALK to his feet)

CONSTANCE

You leave that poor man alone. He's lost his mice, his family and I don't suppose you know anything about that!

Get to Know your Duck

SHERIFF
What? (To Chalk whom he's trying to lift from floor) Did you teach my little girl to sass her daddy?

STEVEN
(Apologetic) Sheriff, she's upset because she lost her squirt.

CONSTANCE
(Blocking Sheriff from Chalk) I can handle this, Steven. Daddy, a woman does not get taught to sass, she gets driven to it by bullies! It's (this is a new word for her) instinctual. We have to protect our young from predators.

SHERIFF
What's happened to ya, baby? I warned you a girl's mind and books don't mix. There is only one book you should be reading. Now you've done it, you've gone daffy!

TWINS
(The sound of daffy duck)

(SHERIFF has managed to lift CHALK to his feet)

CONSTANCE
Daddy, we've got an oversized duck with two heads that the twins found at the swamp and we're going to prove it's deformed because of the pollution Cow Chemical has been dumping and if you don't like it you can, can...fly south!

(SHERIFF drops CHALK to the floor)

SHERIFF
What? What about this duck, Steven?

STEVEN
It's a little... big...

Get to Know your Duck

CHALK
It's as big as I am! It just knocked me down!

STEVEN & CONSTANCE
It did!?

SHERIFF
I'm not talking to you Chalk. (To Steven) What about its head?

STEVEN
Well, it needs a little dental work and...there's...two...

SHERIFF
Two heads?

STEVEN
Yea...only two.

    (DUCK's heads, even bigger, appear in the window where they begin tapping with there beaks)

SHERIFF
Oh, duck poop! (Edging toward door) Two heads...

STEVEN
And an overbite, but it's eating just fine...

    (SHERIFF backs toward door)

SHERIFF
Chalk, I'll get you for contaminating my daughter.

    (SHERIFF EXITS frantically)

CONSTANCE
(Shocked at herself) I talked back to my father.

Get to Know your Duck

STEVEN
That must be why he's upset.

CONSTANCE
Steven. Look out the window. Look at the size. Count the heads.

CHALK
I better go hide him, every one will be after him soon.

STEVEN
After him? I hate to say this, but you're sounding a little paranoid. Why would anyone...? Listen, I agree there's a...question, but...

CONSTANCE
Steven, don't you see what's going on? We've got a predicament here.

STEVEN
Predicament?

CHALK
More of a plight.

STEVEN
Plight?

CONSTANCE
And a quandary.

STEVEN
Quandary?

CHALK
A proverbial imbroglio.

STEVEN
Imbroglio? Isn't that an Italian restaurant?

Get to Know your Duck

CONSTANCE
No, it's a confused heap. A mess. Steven, we're in a mess. The world's in a mess. The ducks in a mess!

STEVEN
Constance, what's happened to you? Up until last night, you couldn't remember what you'd done during the day or what you were cooking for dinner or the names of your children. Now you're...

CONSTANCE
You noticed?

STEVEN
You once asked me if I'd come to read the water meter.

CONSTANCE
But, you never said anything.

STEVEN
I thought you'd get better, maybe there'd be a pill...

CONSTANCE
That's it! The pills! I didn't take any pills last night. I remember now, my memory started going bad on November sixth, my senior year in high school. It was just before the senior prom, I was depressed because I didn't have a date. The doctor gave me Go-Aloft, an anti-depressive medicine. I did poorly on my trigonometry final, a C as I recall, I missed easy calculations on the second, third and seventh problems, but I didn't care because my big smile got me a date for the prom. I wore a pink dress, we bought it at Dundee's Department store from a clerk named Charleen, she wrapped it in...

STEVEN
Constance, you have your memory back!

(STEVEN hugs her)

Get to Know your Duck

CONSTANCE

And I've been taking pills ever since---first for depression, then birth control, and acne, then back pain, and for sleep---You should have said something.

STEVEN

I couldn't, I...I...

TWINS

Cluck, cluck, cluck, cluck.

STEVEN

Yes, I was chicken. Gradually, over the years, I saw you getting worse. I didn't want to face it.

CONSTANCE

And I got even worse when I added the fertility pill.

CHALK

Of course, mixing hormones and sedatives---like testosterone and beer---it makes you really stupid.

STEVEN

It's good to have you back, darling.

> (They embrace and kiss. DUCK taps on window again until a small pane breaks)

DUCK

Quack. Quack.

TWINS

Duck. Duck.

STEVEN

He'll cut himself.

Get to Know your Duck

(STEVEN goes to window and clears away broken glass)

CONSTANCE
Oh, we should give him a name.

TWINS
Humpty. Humpty.

CHALK
Fine symbolism, kids

STEVEN
Hi Humpty. Watch out for the broken glass.

CHALK
.But we are all going to have a great fall and break into sludge if the swamp doesn't get cleaned up.

CONSTANCE
We could call someone at city hall to help. Do you know the mayor?

CHALK
Yes, Fred Holstein, you know, Mr. Cow's brother. Don't get me started on campaign finance reform.

CONSTANCE
(She has something on her mind) There's, the press.

CHALK
The, so called free press. Free! Free? Fee to ignore me! (With Megaphone) It's not free, just priced to sell.

(CHALK, winded by the effort, begins COUGHING, then collapses)

Get to Know your Duck

STEVEN & CONSTANCE

Professor!

CHALK

(Gasping) Don't worry about me. We've got to do something about Humpty. (Wheeze) They'll be back.

(They help CHALK sit)

CONSTANCE

I already did it.

STEVEN

What?

CONSTANCE

When daddy was here I called the TV news office and told them about Humpty.

CHALK

They'll never listen. TV news is controlled by giant corporations ...

CONSTANCE

They talked to me.

CHALK

(Dismayed) They never returned my calls...

CONSTANCE

They're coming.

STEVEN

When?

(The doorbell rings)

Get to Know your Duck

CONSTANCE
Now.

RADON
Cough, wheeze.

STEVEN
Roll over, bowser.

CHALK
(Wheezing. Confused) Ladies and gentlemen...students, today's class...

(CHALK falls asleep)
(DOORBELL rings)

STEVEN
He's fallen asleep.

CONSTANCE
Better let him rest. I'll get the door.

(DOORBELL rings)

TWINS
Visitor. Visitor.

STEVEN
Maybe it's the sheriff, coming back to apologize.

CONSTANCE
Oh!

(Quickly, CONSTANCE pushes STEVEN behind door, puts an umbrella in his hand and has him raise the umbrella over his head. Before he can say anything, she opens door. CLARA FRY ENTERS)

Get to Know your Duck

CLARA
Hello, I'm Clara Fry, the photogenic journalist from K.N.O.D.E.

TWINS
Make-up. Make-up.

CLARA
Are you Constance Bland?

CONSTANCE
Yes.

CLARA
Honest features, wholesome dress. (To outside) OK, boys, set up the equipment. (To Constance) I understand you have an unusual pet story.

CONSTANCE
I'm so glad to see you! Come in, please.

CLARA
Adequate lighting. Thank you.

CONSTANCE
Humpty's not really an unusual pet. He is unusual...

CLARA
Humpty (she begins to take notes), cute name. I'm sure he's very special to you, Connie. Mind if I call you Connie? It's a little more identifiable.

CONSTANCE
Oh, you don't even have to use me at all...

> (CLARA becomes aware of STEVEN holding the umbrella over his head as if to strike)

Get to Know your Duck

STEVEN
(Sheepishly) Hi.

(STEVEN does a little dance with the umbrella)

CLARA
(Jaded) This isn't Humpty is it?

CONSTANCE
Oh, no, this is my husband, he's a man. Humpty is a duck.

CLARA
Listen, I do a show called Unusual Pets, I don't do unusual husbands.

CONSTANCE
Unusual Pets?

CLARA
Yes, if you have an unusual pet we are prepared to go on the air live in five minutes. If not, the station runs a tape on how to enhance your personality. (to Steven) Which shouldn't be taken to extremes, sir.

(STEVEN puts the umbrella down)

CLARA (cont)
Now, I drove all the way out here and I've never done a duck before. I'd like to do your pet, if you are able to cooperate.

STEVEN
My wife has this idea that...

CONSTANCE
(Interrupting, sweetly) We've got the cutest little duck in the world and we'd love to talk about him on live TV.

CLARA
Fine. (To Steven) And you'll wait here...?

Get to Know your Duck

STEVEN
(As if to say OK) Roger.

CLARA
Thank you, Roger.

CONSTANCE
Right this way to the garage, Ms. Fry.

CLARA
Excellent. Now a few questions: Is it a he? How old is he? What does he eat? Does he do any tricks? Does he have any unusual characteristics?

(CLARA and CONSTANCE EXIT)
(STEVEN turns on TV)

TWINS
Action. Action.

TV
(A commercial for The Cow Chemical Company) Cow Chemical, at home, at work and at play, we have the polymer for your needs. And quality? You can be sure if it's a Cow.

NEWS ANCHOR
Welcome back to the news at six. Before Neck Bradshaw's sports report we have a live Unusual Pets segment from the little town of Cowberg. What have you found for us tonight Clara Fry?

CLARA
Thanks, Randy. Tonight I'm talking with Connie Bland who has an unusual feathered pet.

(HUMPTY'S two heads seen behind CLARA)

Get to Know your Duck

CLARA
Before we introduce Humpty the Duck, tell us how you decided on a duck for a pet. Why not a cockatoo, Connie?

CONSTANCE
Are we live on TV?

CLARA
Don't be shy, sweety.

> (CONSTANCE grabs the microphone and speaks super fast)

CONSTANCE
Give me that, you idiot! (To the camera) I don't have a cute pet to show you, I have a mutant, deformed duck with two heads and he's big and getting bigger by the minute because his chromosomes got messed up by toxic chemicals in the pond that's owned by Cow Chemical. And were going to start having human babies like this if we don't do something. Look at him. He would never be recognized by his parents, much less an ornithologist.

> (TV shows HUMPTY who, during Constance's speech, moves closer to the camera. At the same time, some of HUMPTY'S actions can be seen through the living-room windows. He's huge)

STEVEN
(Startled at his size) Humpty? Professor, look!

CONSTANCE
Cow Chemical is distorting the natural cycle into a time warp in which we are not going to be able to survive. The whole cycle is being thrown off because we synthesize-polymerize-manufacture-wear-out-disregard-and then it takes 10,000 years for this stuff to decay. We're creating a cycle that we will not fit into! Think, if the ancient Egyptians had carried water in

Get to Know your Duck

plastic bottles we would be up to our eyeballs in plastic bottles now and 99% of them would be cracked and won't hold water! And, in another 10 years there probably won't be an uncontaminated drop of water left to carry anyway. Soon ducks will be on the endangered species list, along with the over 800 other endangered animals, then on the protected species list, then on the extinct list. Finally the food cycle will collapse and there won't be anyone to keep the extinct list going, which I guess will make the extinct list extinct.

(The screen goes dead, then the anchor comes back on)

TV ANCHOR
(Nervously) Thank you Clara Fry for that Unusual Pet story on the Cowberg Duck. And now...uh, of course, now sports...

(STEVEN turns TV off)
(CONSTANCE ENTERS)
(CHALK wakes and staggers to his feet)

TWINS
Mommy, Mommy, prime time, prime time.

CONSTANCE
I don't think so, kids.

CHALK
Did I miss anything?

STEVEN
(Distraught) My wife, she's turned into a TV terrorist.

CHALK
Good!

Get to Know your Duck

CONSTANCE
Steven, isn't this making any sense to you yet?

STEVEN
Darling, look what's happened. Excuse me, but this...man comes here and the next thing I know you're trespassing on TV, libeling my employer, hanging out with freaks...

TWINS
Hey! Hey!

DUCK
Quack! Quack!

STEVEN
...and giving up on my squirt.

CONSTANCE
No, Steven, I love you. I love my family, but there's a larger family...

(DOORBELL RINGS)

RADON
Cough. Wheeze.

STEVEN
Heel boy. Now who?

CHALK
Probably the sheriff! I'm ready for him.

(CHALK slumps to floor)
(STEVEN opens door. TELEGRAPH PERSON (TP) ENTERS, notes, with suspicion, CHALK on floor)

TP
Steven Bland?

Get to Know your Duck

STEVEN
Yes.

TP
Telegram, sir. (Dramatic music)

CONSTANCE, STEVEN & CHALK
Telegram? (Dramatic music)

TP
(Looking around for the source of the music) You were expecting a FAX?

STEVEN
No.

TP
Sorry to disappoint you. No flowers, no balloons, I don't sing and I get to keep my clothes on.

(STEVEN takes the telegram, signs for it)

STEVEN
Thank you for keeping your clothes on.

TP
You're very welcome, sir. Hope it's not bad news, sir.

STEVEN
For me? Don't be silly.

TP
Oh, I won't sir.

(TELEGRAM PERSON EXITS)

Get to Know your Duck

STEVEN
(Opening TELEGRAM) It's from my boss, Mr. Cow (Dramatic music)

CONSTANCE & CHALK
Mr. Cow? (Dramatic music)

STEVEN
(To music) Stop that, it makes me nervous!. (To Constance and Chalk) He's coming here with an agent from the Environmental Protection Agency.

CONSTANCE
When?

STEVEN
Soon.

(DOORBELL RINGS)

STEVEN (cont.)
Now.

RADON
Cough. Wheeze.

STEVEN
Radon, it's Mr. Cow.

TWINS
Moo. Moo.

CHALK
Cow! Cow!? That pig! That porcine bovine! I've been trying to fight it out with that ...

CONSTANCE
No, wait. What if it's a trap?

Get to Know your Duck

CHALK
A trap?

CONSTANCE
A trap. Any stratagem designed to catch or trick.

CHALK
A ducknapping?

(DOORBELL RINGS)

CONSTANCE
Quick. Let's hide Humpty in the fallout shelter!

CHALK
Fallout shelter? Everyone knows that fallout shelters would be useless for a thermonuclear event. In fact the...

STEVEN
Wait. Wait...

(DOORBELL rings. CONSTANCE grabs CHALK and heads for the kitchen)

CONSTANCE
Remember the mice? Humpty's our last chance.

CHALK
You're right, a Cow will stop at nothing.

(CHALK EXITS. Just as CONSTANCE is about to leave...)

STEVEN
Wait a minute. This is my boss, he's a good Cow.

Get to Know your Duck

(CONSTANCE stops and turns to STEVEN)

CONSTANCE
(Pleading) Stevey...

STEVEN
Darling, if there's something wrong with the swamp, Mr. Cow will do something about it, he's grade A all the way.

(DOORBELL RINGS)

COW (OS)
Steven? Are you home?

STEVEN
(Smiling at Constance) I'll get it.

(As STEVEN turns to open door, CONSTANCE hides behind couch [still seen by audience]. STEVEN opens door. Wall of smog enters)

COW
Hello, Steven. So glad to find you home.

TWINS
Moo, moo.

(COW and ORANGE enter wearing gas masks)

STEVEN
Mr. Cow, I'm glad you're here.

COW
(Removing gasmask) Good, good. I'm very grateful to you for inviting me on such short notice.

Get to Know your Duck

STEVEN
I was just on my way to work.

COW
Excellent, excellent. You are a little late---no problem, of course---I know you have a family, things come up, a fine employee like yourself, but I thought I'd check and Mr. Orange came along. Mr. Orange is an agent with the Environmental Protection Agency.

STEVEN
I think I've heard of your work, Agent Orange.

ORANGE
I'm flattered. Gosh, you have a nice town here.

STEVEN
This is your first visit?

ORANGE
Yes. But I'd like to come more often. (He smiles at Cow)

(COW wipes his feet on RADON)

RADON
Cough. Wheeze.

TWINS
Radon! Radon!

STEVEN
(To RADON) Sit, you rascal.

(ORANGE sits on command)

COW
Cowberg. Our home town. Home town America. Where we live and prosper.

Get to Know your Duck

STEVEN
And raise our families.

COW
Indeed, and raise our families, so that they too can compete in the marketplace. Now, there's nothing wrong is there?

STEVEN
No, of course not. I did want to talk with you...

COW
Fine, fine. Now, I have my car out front, what if I give you a lift into work? We'll just go take care of our little business and leave Agent Orange to take care of his government work.

STEVEN
Government work?

COW
Yes, thank God for bureaucrats, right? He'll take care of everything around here. Shall we? (Indicating the door)

STEVEN
Take care of what everything?

COW
Of course, we heard about the duck problem.

STEVEN
Oh, it's not exactly a duck problem. I mean, he's got problems, but...

ORANGE
I understand he's unique.

STEVEN
Unique, yes, but it's not his fault.

Get to Know your Duck

COW
Of course, of course, nobody's assigning blame. You know my philosophy; problems are solutions waiting to happen. We have a problem, we find a solution. No blame, no wrong, only answers.

STEVEN
That's right! Answers. No blame, right. And there are questions...

COW
Excellent. Let's go resolve those paperwork questions at the office.

STEVEN
OK. (To Orange) Oh, we named him Humpty. And, you know, I think he knows his name.

COW
Mr. Orange will have a solution and he'll take care of all the paper shuffling. Is this your coat?

STEVEN
Yes. (To Orange) Ah, he is friendly, you knew that?

COW
We are running a little late, Steven.

STEVEN
I'm sorry. I was just wondering, the duck is funny, I admit, not funny ha ha, but, definitely altered, and he lived in the swamp...

COW
Mr. Orange is a servant of our government. He's a specialist with wildfowl.

STEVEN
Humpty's a little sloppy, but he's not really foul.

Get to Know your Duck

COW
Isn't it wonderful how we all work together to make this big world run smoother?

STEVEN
Yes, wonderful. So, you're not worried about the swamp?

COW
I believe it'll fetch a hefty price.

STEVEN
Well, no, I meant...

COW
Steven, we really do need to be running along. Have you ever ridden in my limousine?

STEVEN
Wow. No. Sure, I'm ready.

(CONSTANCE, unseen by all, stands and starts to speak)

TWINS
Dead duck. Dead duck.

(CONSTANCE hides)

STEVEN
(To Orange) Excuse me, I'd kind of like to know, Agent Orange, what will you be doing with Humpty?

COW
Very good. I respect frankness. Let me be frank.

STEVEN
And I respect a frank cow. Sir, he's just a poor duck, with some minor problems. He's kind of cute and affectionate.

Get to Know your Duck

COW
A man with a heart, I like that.

STEVEN
(To Orange) You'll take good care of Humpty?

ORANGE
(Referring to his briefcase) I just have a few papers for you to sign...

STEVEN
I'm not really interested in the papers. Do you know about Humpty's problems?

ORANGE
No problems, with the proper papers...

COW
Mr. Bland knows paper work. He's done a fine job, in the past, for Cow Chemical.

ORANGE
Oh, a fellow paper pusher. (Rotating both hands in the air) I can push with both hands.

(CONSTANCE stands, unseen by all, and starts to speak)

TWINS
Bureaucrat. Bureaucrat.

(CONSTANCE hides)

STEVEN
Ah, well, I'm not shuffling papers right now. I...I always sort of minded my own business. I scanned the newspaper. I paid my taxes. I followed the rules---even read the small print. But, now there's this situation and Humpty and a swamp and Bambi and, well...We need some answers, right?

Get to Know your Duck

ORANGE
(Not knowing what else to say, he pulls a form from his briefcase) Forms, we need forms, I have a form D-2292...

COW
Steven, I'm a man who likes a man who likes to talk.

STEVEN
I'm a man who likes to talk to a man who likes to listen.

ORANGE
That's D, as in duck,...

COW
I'm a man who likes a man who likes to talk to a man who likes to listen.

STEVEN
I'm a man who likes a man who likes to talk to a man who likes to listen to a man who likes to talk.

COW
I'm your man, because I like a man who likes to talk to a man who likes to listen to a man who likes to talk.

ORANGE
(Pulling out a very long form) This form, if you'd care to sign here, allows us to use the reduced paper-work in government form...

COW
Steven, if you are a man who likes to talk to a man who likes to listen, then I am listening. I'm a reasonable man. What do you want for the duck?

STEVEN
(To COW) Excuse me, Mr. Cow, I don't want anything, I...

Get to Know your Duck

COW
Now, now, don't be coy. I understand business.

STEVEN
I'm not coy, Cow. I just want Humpty to be safe and for there to be an investigation.

COW
Investigation? Oh, of course. Good. Good. Yes. Agent Orange will get right on that.

ORANGE
On what?

STEVEN
(To Orange) And inspections. If this is the first time you've been to Cowberg, how are inspections done?

ORANGE
Inspections? No, no, no. No more big government interfering with business. We no longer waste taxpayer's money peeking over the shoulder of industry.

COW
A wise tax savings.

>(CHALK, unseen by all, pushes door open and starts to speak, but stops as...)

TWINS
Cover up. Cover up.

(CHALK EXITS)

STEVEN
I suppose, yes. But what about...doesn't that sort of leave business free to...

Get to Know your Duck

COW
Steven, this is wonderful. I admire your curiosity. Curiosity is a fine trait in a potential manager.

STEVEN
Manager? Wow, you never said anything...

COW
I've been watching you. You're a bright young man. Curiosity, that's good. And loyalty, that's better.

STEVEN
Oh course, sir.

COW
I knew you were loyal. (Serious) Now, no more delays.

STEVEN
Yes. OK. (Putting on his coat)

(CHALK, unseen by all, ENTERS and starts to speak)

TWINS
Three mile island. Three mile island.

(CHALK EXITS)

STEVEN
So, something will be done? Someone's taking care of the environment?

ORANGE
Mr. Cow takes care of the business environment and I take care of the paper environment.

STEVEN
No, I mean the ecology.

Get to Know your Duck

ORANGE
Ecology? Sorry?

STEVEN
You know, the land and water and plants and animals, how they all live together.

ORANGE
Ah, socialism! Now that was a silly idea, wasn't it?

STEVEN
I wouldn't know about that. But, there is Humpty and he's got problems which may be related to the environment.

COW
(Steering Steven toward door) Thinking about the problems of others, that's admirable. I didn't know you were such a caring kind of guy. That's special. You know, Steven, I see a therapist, I have feeling too. I had one just the other day. We should do lunch sometime.

STEVEN
Thank you sir. But, Agent Orange, I want you to let me know if anything shows up. I'm interested in hearing.

ORANGE
Are you requesting a hearing. I have a request for hearing form here...

STEVEN
No. I just want to make sure Humpty's alright. Do you know about his special needs?

ORANGE
Oh, my God, he doesn't need handicap access does he?

STEVEN
No. Not exactly. But, I think there's something wrong.

Get to Know your Duck

COW
Steven, Steven, Steven, nothing's wrong. Remember, no wrong, no blame, only solutions. Let Agent Orange do his work and we'll do ours. Everything is fine.

(CHALK ENTERS about to speak)

STEVEN
(Sounding like Chalk) Fine? Fine?

(CHALK EXITS)

STEVEN (cont.)
Excuse me, things aren't exactly fine. There's a few strange things going on around here. May I ask, why are you in such a hurry to sell the swamp, sir?

ORANGE
Shall I call in the other agents, sir?

STEVEN
What other agents?

COW
No, no, no. It isn't necessary. Mr Bland is our friend, an American, he's given up time from his family to listen and cooperate. You are willing to cooperate with your country, aren't you, Steven?

STEVEN
Right. Of course. I'm here to cooperate. I just...

(ENGINE NOISES outside. STEVEN looks out window)

STEVEN (cont.)
There are bulldozers out there! Why?

Get to Know your Duck

COW
Steven, you are a man of determination. I'm a man who likes a man of...

STEVEN
Please, sir, I'm trying to talk to Mr. Orange. (To ORANGE) I'm a taxpayer, I am asking you to watch out for Humpty's and my family's welfare. No shuffling papers to make things look legal, no illegal polluting.

COW
I beg your pardon, I think Mr. Orange will certify that Cow Chemical does not pollute illegally.

ORANGE
No, they have all the proper forms.

STEVEN
I'm sure that's true, and I didn't mean any offense, but I've heard there's maybe some dumping of toxic chemicals in the swamp and that mice eating...

COW
That's the theory of a crackpot! He has no evidence. There's not a single mouse that'll testify against a Cow.

STEVEN
How do you know the mice are missing?

COW
You do like to talk, don't you? I'm a man who doesn't like a man who talks too much.

STEVEN
(To Orange) One thing I don't understand, do you work for Cow Chemical?

Get to Know your Duck

ORANGE
Yes. I mean no. Well, not yet anyway. (He smiles at Cow)

STEVEN
You're here to protect the public, right?

ORANGE
I process papers from all sides equally.

STEVEN
But, I don't have any papers!

ORANGE
That's O.K., Mr. Cow's provided me with plenty of papers.

STEVEN
Do you even know what this poor duck looks like?

ORANGE
Doesn't matter. Equal opportunity. No discrimination based on race, color...

STEVEN
Number of heads?

COW
Steven, let me try and make this as painless as possible. We are willing to offer you (he takes an envelope from his coat) a sizable 'reward' for finding the duck.

ORANGE
Yes, as part of the EPA's endangered species recovery act...

STEVEN
(To Cow) Thank's, but I...a reward? I don't know. I could use some extra money.

Get to Know your Duck

COW
Imagine what you could buy.

(CONSTANCE, unseen, stands and starts to speak)

TWINS
Ice cream. Ice cream.

(CONSTANCE, startled by what she's heard, hides)

COW
This reward could straighten a lot of teeth.

STEVEN
Yes, that's what I was thinking.

COW
Yes. And feet.

STEVEN
Feet?

COW
Yes. And fertilize a lot of little Blands.

STEVEN
Fertilizer?

ORANGE
Fertilizer falls under the farm subsidy program...

COW
(Showing the envelope) What do you say, Steven?

Get to Know your Duck

(CONSTANCE, unseen, stands and looks desperately at Steven)

STEVEN
I say....uhm...I say...

COW
I'm a man who doesn't trust a man who says he can't be "rewarded."

TWINS
Slug meat. Slug meat.

STEVEN
(Increasingly angry) Are you planning on making Humpty into slug meat?

(CONSTANCE is horrified)

ORANGE
Meat is the responsibility of the Food and Drug Administrations.

COW
No more delays, turn the bird over!

STEVEN
And let you make duck pate'?

ORANGE
Pate'? Is that under the Federal School Lunch Program?

COW
Think, Steven, haven't you ever been in a situation where people panic? If this duck gets out people will panic in the street. Everything is under control now, our environment is being protected by the government with the cooperation of industry...

Get to Know your Duck

STEVEN
Under control? Professor Chalk says there are a million toxic waste dumps, that 95% of the water table is contaminated...

COW
(Sounding like Chalk) Chalk! Chalk! That liberal tree humper! That...

(CHALK, hearing his name, ENTERS unseen. CONSTANCE pushes CHALK out. He EXITS. She hides)

STEVEN
... even the oceans are polluted. Do you call that control? Maybe people should be in the streets!

ORANGE
A street permit? That's up to your local authority...

STEVEN
And protection? Mr. Orange, did you know that air is suppose to be clear and odorless?

ORANGE
Not according to EPA standards.

STEVEN
Mr. Cow, do you even care about the swamp, the mice, Humpty, or my children?

COW
It is obvious that you, sir, are a subversive. If you loved your country you would love Cow Chemical and all the politicians we pay for.

STEVEN
(Beside himself in anger) Sir, you.... You are....You are a (cringing to say it) negative person.

(CONSTANCE, unseen, stands, smiling at Steven)

Get to Know your Duck

COW
That's it! Shut up, lackey, and hand the bird over!

STEVEN
(A difficult word for Steven) N...N...N...

(CONSTANCE mouths the word "No")

TWINS
Ice cream! Ice cream!

STEVEN
No. No! NO! There, I can say it! NO!

COW
No? What about your job?

STEVEN
Nnn... My job?

COW
The ear tubes, the orthotics, the braces...

(CONSTANCE, standing behind COW, is about to hit him with the Smog-O-Matic, when STEVEN sees her and holds up his hand for her to stop)

STEVEN
How did you...? (Calmly) Mr. Cow, I always thought you were a blue ribbon Cow, but now I see you're just after money. And, I don't want a job that helps create ecological disaster.

COW
Yes, but ecological disaster with a 401-k.

Get to Know your Duck

STEVEN
Please leave.

ORANGE
(To COW) Hey, can I have his job?

COW
(To Steven) You don't get it, do you? We came for the roast duck and we're not leaving until you serve it.

STEVEN
No! NO! Out!

ORANGE
But, you haven't signed a single form...

STEVEN
(With MEGAPHONE) Out! Out!

COW
You can't throw me out! I'll grind you up like I did those mice!

(CHALK come in running)

CHALK
Mice!

COW
Chalk!

CHALK
Cow!

(CHALK and COW face off as wrestlers)

TWINS
Fight! Fight!

Get to Know your Duck

ORANGE
(Reciting) Ah, ah, I'm only doing my job. Would you like to speak with my superior? I'm only doing my job. Would you like to speak with my superior? I'm only...(etc., as)

CHALK
Cow, you swine!

COW
Well, well, Professor Chalk, my arch enemy.

STEVEN
Have you tried orthotics?

> (Just as CHALK and COW are about to start fighting, STEVEN takes the Smog-O-Matic. CONSTANCE opens the door)

STEVEN
(Turning on the Smog-O-Matic) Out, out of my house!

> (COW and ORANGE EXIT hurriedly. CONSTANCE slams the door behind them)

COW
Call in the bulldozers!

CHALK
I could have taken him. I'd turn him into hamburger. I'd... (coughing overtakes him)

CONSTANCE
Steven, you were wonderful.

STEVEN
Oh my. I lost my job. Do you think I was too...rude...too...I feel strange.

Get to Know your Duck

CONSTANCE
No, no, you weren't too, you were just right. (She kisses him passionately)

STEVEN
Wow! Did you hear what I said? No. NO! I feel good. Great! Exhilarated! Like I'm breathing pure oxygen---O2---the kind without coloring! What happened?

STEVEN
And that was some kiss. How about another?

(The kiss a long time while...)

CHALK
(Sitting. Short of breath) Probably the effect of adrenal hormones on the lungs and diaphragm. (Catching his breath) Your confrontation with Cow triggered an adrenaline release which stimulates the breathing... (cough)

CONSTANCE
Steven, I feel like my uterus is round and open.

CHALK
Now that would be due to the release of...

CONSTANCE
I don't think we'll need a specimen container anymore.

STEVEN
Darling...

(A helicopter is heard overhead)

MEGAPHONE VOICE FROM HELICOPTER
Everyone out of the house with your hands up.

Get to Know your Duck

CONSTANCE

What's that?

TWINS

Visitors. Visitors.

MEGAPHONE VOICE

We have the house surrounded. Do as you are told and nobody will be hurt.

TWINS

Big, oink! Big, oink!

CHALK

It's the SQUAT team!

MEGAPHONE VOICE

We know you have the duck down there.

CONSTANCE

Humpty!

CHALK

We've got to act fast!

(CHALK sets up his barrel of swamp water)

CONSTANCE

What do we do?

MEGAPHONE VOICE

Send the duck out with it's wings in the air.

STEVEN

Professor, what are you doing?

Get to Know your Duck

CHALK
(Flicking on a lighter) Observe, this metal canister is filled with swamp water. Attached to it is a fuse. In my hand is a flame...

>(CONSTANCE and STEVEN dive into hiding, protecting the TWINS)

CONSTANCE
No!

CHALK
It's all over, we might as well go out with a bang.

STEVEN
Wait!

>(They all stop)

STEVEN
I have an idea.

>(Bugle call)

CONSTANCE
An idea?

>(Bugle call)

CHALK
(Looking around for bugles) An idea, a thought or notion or...Am I hearing bugles?

STEVEN
What about the cavalry?

Get to Know your Duck

CHALK
You're out of your century.

STEVEN
What about getting them to help? (He points to the audience)

CONSTANCE
Them?

STEVEN
Yes.

CHALK
Brilliant, we'll take them as hostages! (Into megaphone he yells out the window) One step closer and I'll blow the audience up!

STEVEN
No, no, maybe they can think of some way of helping?

CHALK
Some cavalry, I used to have faith in them but... Look, they've been sitting all evening.

STEVEN
If the Blands can learn to act, so can they.

(Helicopter roars louder)
(The giant heads of HUMPTY can now be seen looking in. They fill the entire window)

MEGAPHONE VOICE
This is your last chance. All members of the Duck Liberation Army are to come out with your hands up or we will blow your house up.

(MRS. LEXIA enters running)

Get to Know your Duck

LEXIA

There's a loose on the duck. Everyone, run! Duck giant. Run! Run! It's the world of the end as we know! It's the world of the end as we know! Run! There's a loose on the duck!

(MRS. LEXIA EXITS)

TWINS

Visitor. Visitor.

(HELICOPTER heard passing overhead.)

CHALK

That gives me an idea. Observe, the canister. (He turns canister on it's side) Open the door.

(CONSTANCE opens the door)

CHALK (cont.)

Observe, flame.

(CHALK flicks on lighter, lights the fuse and kicks canister which rolls out the door. CONSTANCE shuts the door. Outside, an EXPLOSION, then the sound of the ENGINE CHOKING, then it dies)

STEVEN

What's happened?

CHALK

(Looking out the window, speaking calmly) An internal combustion engine requires oxygen. The explosion temporarily removed all oxygen from the air. (Yelling) Everyone down!

(STEVEN and CONSTANCE jump to cover the TWINS. CHALK falls to the floor. Crash of helicopter outside.

Get to Know your Duck

House shakes. A portion of ceiling falls in allowing outside light into room)

SQUAT TEAM VOICES (outside)
What happened? Are you OK, Butch? (Etc)

HUMPTY (outside)
(Very deep voice) Quack, quack, quack.

SQUAT TEAM VOICES (outside)
What the hell is that? Look out! Watch out! Run!
(SQUAT team can be seen running past the window, HUMPTY in pursuit)

CHALK
(Looking out window) Zippidy-do! I think we won the battle!

(POUNDING on the door)

SHERIFF (outside)
Steven, Constance, open this door, I'm going to arrest you. Do you hear?

(CONSTANCE opens the door. SHERIFF ENTERS)

SHERIFF (cont)
Sin, sin, sin! You're all sinners. And you have the right to remain silent.

STEVEN
I see that I have been silent far too long. Sheriff, what about your duty to protect this duck.

SHERIFF
Oh, rabbit pellets.

HUMPTY
(From above) Quack, quack.

Get to Know your Duck

(They ALL look up through the hole in the ceiling)

SHERIFF
Holy duck shiiiitttt!

(SHERIFF is dumped on by HUMPTY. He's buried in it. He remains stuck to the floor where he continues struggling)

TWINS
Bad word. Bad word.

SHERIFF
Someone upstairs is going to hear about this.

CHALK
We had better start moving Humpty toward Washington D.C.

STEVEN
I'll see about renting a flat-bed truck.

(MR. COW ENTERS)

COW
Good. Good. How fortunate I found you at home. I'm a man who likes a family that can be found at home.

(MR. ORANGE ENTERS.)

ORANGE
Mr. Cow, I was wondering about that job you promised me.

COW
(Stage whisper) Get me the head of that duck and you can have anything.

Get to Know your Duck

ORANGE
Me? But, boss...

COW
Don't call me boss. (To Steven) Steven, name your price for the little waddle?

STEVEN
I'm sorry, Mr. Cow, no duck.

ORANGE
(On his hands and knees at Cow's feet) Please, please, please give me his job.

COW
(To Orange) No. Away with you. (Inching his way toward Chalk) Steven, Steven, be reasonable, wasn't I always good to you?

(COW grabs CHALK from behind and pulls out a vial)

COW (cont.)
Everyone back! This vial is full of concentrated swamp water!

EVERYONE
Gasp!

COW
(Holding Chalk) Anyone moves and I toss it in his face! It'll eat him alive!

STEVEN & CONSTANCE
No! You can't!

COW
Yes I can! I hold the patent! It's what I sell as carburetor cleaner.

CONSTANCE
Please...

Get to Know your Duck

COW
Where's the duck?

CHALK
(Struggling) A Cow doesn't scare me!

ORANGE
(Attaching himself to COW'S leg) Please, please. I'll do anything to have this job. I'll even work.

COW
(Trying to shake ORANGE off his leg) Off, off, you parasite. (To STEVEN) Give me the duck or Chalk's toast.

(With ORANGE distracting COW, CHALK breaks free leaving COW and ORANGE together. Orange remains attached to Cow's leg pleading)

ORANGE
(Pleading) I worked once before. Really, I did. I...

HUMPTY
(From above, very deep voice) Quack, quack.

(ALL look around)

TWINS
Look up! Look up!

(ALL look up)

COW
(Looking through the hole in the ceiling) Ahh!! Nice ducky.

ORANGE
Stop! I'm a civil servant! You're off your leash.

Get to Know your Duck

COW
(Pleading) I'm a man who likes a duck who likes a man who...

(HUMPTY'S webbed foot enters and crushes COW and ORANGE)

TWINS
Fallen arches! Fallen arches!

STEVEN
(To Chalk) Never mind the truck, I think we'll have to walk to the legislature.

(CHALK inspects Humpty's fallen arches)

CONSTANCE
(Going to Twins) Are my baby's OK?

TWINS
Duck. Duck.

HUMPTY
Quack. Quack.

STEVEN   CONSTANCE
Sweetheart.   Darling.

(They embrace)

CHALK
(Looking in BUCKET) Are these the slugs the twins gathered?

CONSTANCE
Yes. (To twins) My lovely twins.

Get to Know your Duck

(CHALK reaches into the bucket and lifts out a three foot long slug with two heads)

CHALK
Kind of cute for a mutant, eh?

(A bar of DRAMATIC MUSIC)
(HUMPTY looks in window)
(Sound of BULLDOZERS starting up)

TWINS
Peterbilt. Peterbilt.

STEVEN
It's the bulldozers!

HUMPTY
Quack. Quack.

RADON
Cough. Wheeze.

STEVEN
(To audience) We need your help stopping this! If you don't care about the Spotted Owl or the Snow Leopard or the Imperial Eagle, then think about your children. What if every one of us took a photo of our children and mailed it to your Senator or Congress-person? Take a family photo and on the back of it write your representatives name and address and below the picture of your children write "Endangered species, save their environment."

CONSTANCE
(To audience) And if you don't have children of your own, please consider our children.

Get to Know your Duck

(STEVEN picks up the TWINS from the couch where they have been sitting for the entire play. The TWINS are a two-headed doll with webbed feet. CONSTANCE and STEVEN stand downstage with the TWINS between them. STEVEN combs the TWINS hair)

<u>TWINS</u>

Feet hurt. Feet hurt.

(CHALK joins them downstage and holds up Twin's feet as he looks curiously at them. Then he looks for an answer from Steven and Constance, who seem to notice the webbed feet for the first time)

<u>CONSTANCE & STEVEN</u>

Help!!!!!

<u>DUCK</u>

Quack. Quack.

<u>TWINS</u>

Duck. Duck.

<u>RADON</u>

Bark. Bark.

<u>TWINS</u>

Dog. Dog.

(Etc. as...

(CURTAIN)

3765849

Made in the USA